Andy
Walker

ROY ROGERS
and the
Ghost of Mystery Rancho

An original story featuring
ROY ROGERS
famous motion picture star as the hero

By
WALKER A. TOMPKINS

Illustrated by
ANDREW BENSEN

Authorized Edition

WHITMAN PUBLISHING COMPANY
RACINE, WISCONSIN

CONTENTS

ILLUSTRATIONS

Roy Rogers Looked Out Over Tomahawk Basin

ROY ROGERS
and the
Ghost of Mystery Rancho

CHAPTER I

THE TALKING SKULL

Dropping hands to the butts of Colt six-guns holstered at their flanks, two riders reined up in the sparse shade of a smoke tree overhanging the Old Spanish Trail.

Here on the lofty, sun-parched crown of the Navajada Range, they had a wide view of Tomahawk Basin. Shimmering in the heat of the Texas sun, the Basin was bounded on west, north, and east by the rocky teeth of the mountains, and cut off from Mexico on the south by the deep gorge of the Rio Grande.

It was difficult to realize that this isolated pocket in the Texas Big Bend was a land that harbored death and mystery. It did not seem like a battle-ground where evil forces from south of the border were even now engaged in a death struggle with the Lone Star cattleman whose outfit, the Box C—now known as "Mystery Rancho"—encompassed most of this cliff-rimmed sink.

But such was the case. And it was the pressure of this grim knowledge which had caused Captain John Whetlaw of the far-famed Texas Rangers, as well as the sun-bronzed young cowboy at his stirrup, to drop a hand to holster.

The grizzled old Ranger hipped around in saddle to study the smoke-hazed reaches of the Basin, considering each near-by cactus clump or shadowy gulch as a potential ambush. A long training in trouble had sharpened Whetlaw's senses, alerting him whenever the trail of duty led him into dangerous country.

The sense that this sleepy wasteland harbored peril was strong in the old lawman now, laying its acid taste on his tongue, hardening his jaw under its screening sandy mustache.

"This spot is what Buck Conroy's telegram described as the 'High Gate' in his range boundary." Whetlaw's tired voice broke the run of silence between them. "In the past couple of years two of my Rangers, a deputy U.S. marshal and a Border Patrol inspector have disappeared without trace before reaching Conroy's ranch. That's why he warned me in his wire, Roy, to take this old Spanish Trail cutoff into the Basin, instead of the stagecoach road through Gunsight town."

Roy Rogers cuffed back his dusty gray Stetson and scanned the untamed beauty of these badlands.

Like his flaxen-maned palomino horse, Trigger, Rogers was a picture of rugged, leaned-down fighting power. An unusual chain of events accounted for Rogers being with the Texas Ranger now.

A short week ago he had run into Whetlaw in Alamo Plaza in San Antonio. An old friend of Whetlaw's, young Rogers had jumped at the chance of accompanying the Ranger on what the old man described as the most dangerous assignment of his career. And here they were answering Buck Conroy's call for help at Mystery Rancho.

Now, scanning the wild grandeur of Tomahawk Basin, Rogers found it incredible that this wonderland of lava and cactus held the key to the mysterious fates of four other lawmen, each as fast-shooting and courageous as old John Whetlaw.

"If this so-called 'Ghost of Mystery Rancho' is bent on driving Conroy off his ranch," Roy Rogers commented gravely, "the old man must have had a good reason for wanting our arrival to be a secret, John."

The alkali dust of a long trail across the Texas frontier shook from the sleeve of Rogers's wine-colored rodeo shirt as the handsome young cowboy gestured toward a remote group of barns and corrals down on the basin floor below them.

"If that's Box C," Rogers went on, "we could reach there in an hour's ride from this High Gate.

Or do we wait for dark?"

The old Ranger captain rummaged in a pocket of his calfskin vest and drew forth a soiled telegram which he had received at Ranger headquarters in San Antonio ten days before.

"Conroy says we'll find further instructions," he said, "under a painted rock at the foot of a smoke tree at High Gate. Since this is the only smoke tree in sight of the Spanish Trail, I reckon this is where we pick up Buck's message, Roy."

The two men stepped down from stirrups, moving with the stiff weariness of riders who had been eighteen hours in saddle. Off his horse, Whetlaw made a dried-up figure, stooped by the weight of the long years of riding and shooting which lay behind his Ranger service, scarred by old knife and gun-shot wounds which had crippled him bodily, if not spiritually.

Roy Rogers, on the other hand, loomed huskier off his horse than on it; a rugged young buckaroo of solid bone and muscle testifying to his code of clean living. He was a tall man even without the added height of his custom-made cowboots and high-crowned sombrero.

Circling the gnarled roots of the smoke tree, they found a lava rock, invisible from the trail, at the base of the trunk. The stone carried the time-eroded out-lines of a prehistoric Indian picture on its upper face, identifying it as the "Painted Rock" mentioned in Buck Conroy's telegram.

Roy Rogers felt his heart quicken with excitement as he watched his old Ranger friend hunker down and roll the painted boulder aside. In the shallow hole thus exposed was a tobacco can, showing no rust, and obviously placed there recently.

Opening the can with feverish haste, Whetlaw drew out a single sheet of paper. The old man's watery eyes shuttled over the writing, then handed the paper to Roy Rogers. The message, scrawled in a bold but shaky hand, read:

A hundred yards to the north of where you now stand you will see the old ruins of the "Haunted Mission" of the Spanish padres. I will be waiting for you there on the day you name.

Wear your Ranger star to identify you. If this seems strange, it is because you are even now within the range of the Ghost's guns. We have to play this thing safe.

Buck Conroy

Both men turned to scan the sage-dotted slope which lifted above the north flank of the Old Spanish Trail.

Outlined sharply against the brass-colored skyline, they saw the crumbled adobe bell tower and broken tile roofs and archways of an ancient chapel, which dated back four hundred years to the era when Coronado's armored conquerors had first explored and pillaged this land, in search of the fabulous Seven Cities of Cibola.

"Roy, you wait here on the trail with the horses," Whetlaw said. "Conroy might get scared if I show up with a stranger who doesn't wear a star. From what I understand of this Mystery Rancho business, the old man doesn't know friend from foe. The Ghost might be one of his own men, for all he knows."

Roy Rogers walked back to where Trigger and the other horse stood three-footed in the dust, and loosened the saddle leathers as the Ranger captain set off alone up the flinty slope toward Haunted Mission.

At this high elevation and in the punishing August heat, the old man's over-taxed heart began hammering his ribs by the time he completed the short, steep climb to the ruined chapel.

He worked his way impatiently across a jungle of cactus thickets which marked the mission's old graveyard, marked by the weed-grown crosses and grave mounds of long-dead men.

This ghostly spot was shrouded in gloomy, foreboding silence. As he reached the arched doorway of the Haunted Mission, Whetlaw discovered no sign of life among the ruins other than the noisy swallows who had nested under the tiled eaves.

Unaware that a pair of beady eyes watched his approach from one of the windows in the high bell tower, Whetlaw halted at the dark entrance of the ruined mission. Getting no answer to his call, he believed he had missed connections with the Box C cattleman whom he had telegraphed to meet him here this afternoon at the High Gate.

Then, from somewhere inside the shadow-clotted archway, a ghostly voice greeted him. "John Whetlaw of the Rangers?"

Whetlaw felt cold sweat pop out on his weather-beaten forehead as he heard his name thus called in hollow, unearthly tones. He muttered to himself, ashamed at having fallen under the sinister spell of these grim ruins.

"Yes, I'm Whetlaw," he answered huskily, brushing a palm across the shiny silver star on his vest. "That you, Conroy?"

At that instant, Whetlaw's faded eyes caught sight of a seated human figure directly inside this doorway, not ten feet from where he stood in the ankle-deep weeds by the doorstep.

In the act of stepping through the mission's thick-walled portal, Whetlaw halted stock-still, horror freezing his veins.

The seated figure was not Buck Conroy. Whetlaw was staring at a dead man! The corpse held a rusty

Colt six-gun in either hand, the long barrels resting on chap-clad knees, their bores trained on the doorway where Whetlaw stood.

What was even more incredible, this gruesome figure had been dead a long time for it was mummified. Under the drooping brim of a sombrero, the figure's face was a time-yellowed skull. Cobwebs had been spun in the hollow, staring eye-sockets, and the ghostly hands which clutched the twin .45's were mere claws of leather and bone, like an eagle's feet.

"Conroy," came the ghostly voice from that grinning skull, "is dead, Ranger Whetlaw. And you will die if you attempt to solve the riddle of the Ghost of Mystery Rancho. Take warning and ride!"

Whetlaw swayed on his feet, gripping the broken adobe walls for support. He thought, *This heat's got me. I'm stark crazy. I'm seeing things that couldn't be!*

The Ranger's eyes as well as his ears were tricking him, for the skeleton's jaw had moved as the skull spoke each word!

Even as he stood paralyzed by that voice from the dead, Whetlaw saw the skull's lower jaw move in time with the phantom voice.

"Four other lawmen tried to reach Tomahawk Basin and failed before you came, John Whetlaw. Go back to San Antonio—and tell no one what you have seen or heard here."

John Whetlaw shook himself out of his trance with a supreme effort of will power. He glanced around, sheepish in the guilty knowledge of his cowardice before this supernatural thing.

Down on the Old Spanish Trail, Roy Rogers stood stroking Trigger's velvety muzzle. That much, at least, was solid truth. This talking skull had no reality. It was a figment of his deranged imagination. It had to be. But was it?

Forcing himself to turn back toward the seated skeleton in chaps and Stetson, Whetlaw lifted a gun from leather and thumbed back the hammer to full cock.

"Dead men don't scare Rangers any more than live ones," snarled Whetlaw, half to himself. "If you're this Ghost that Conroy wants laid low, we'll settle that here and now!"

Whetlaw lifted his cocked .45 and lunged forward across the threshold, firing as he did so.

Instantly one of the skeleton's six-guns exploded with a flash of flame and smoke, the recoil jerking the mummy's arm off its knee, then dropping back into its former stiff pose.

Gunsmoke swirling about him, Whetlaw dropped his own gun and groped with both hands to stem the flow of blood which leaked from a bullet hole punched through his chest.

Slowly the Ranger's knees buckled and Whetlaw

fell back into the hot sunshine, his senses wheeling on the verge of a black and bottomless pit of pain.

The crash of double gunshots from Haunted Mission were volleying off along the Navajada divide in echo as Roy Rogers called to his horse, "Wait here, Trigger, till I call you—" and started up the rocky slope at a run.

Those deafening shots told Rogers that Whetlaw had run into danger up on the ridge. For all Roy knew, he might be heading straight into the range of an ambusher's gun, but to desert a friend in time of peril was contrary to the hard-bitten code which had always ruled Rogers's life.

Crossing the mission's cemetery at a run, Roy Rogers skidded to a halt in front of the arched doorway, through which milky streamers of gunpowder smoke still drifted and eddied in the sluggish air currents.

At his feet lay the crumpled form of John Whetlaw, his lifeblood streaming crimson between his fingers.

Leaping to one side, knowing the shot had come from the depths of the mission, Rogers pulled his dying friend to the base of the bell tower and ripped open the old Texan's shirt.

One glance at the bullet hole so close to the heart told Roy that his partner was doomed.

Whetlaw's eyes flickered open. Recognition flamed

in their depths as he stared up at the cowboy.

"The Talkin' Skull . . . shot me," the Ranger's whisper reached Roy Rogers's ears. "Son . . . do me . . . last favor?"

Roy Rogers, keeping an alert eye on the doorway of death, knelt beside the Ranger.

"I'll do anything you ask," vowed the cowboy, his throat aching with grief. "You name it, I promise to do it."

With a trembling, blood-wet fist, John Whetlaw unpinned his Ranger captain's badge. Summoning what strength was left him, the old lawman reached up and affixed the circle-enclosed star to Roy Rogers's shirt.

"Your job . . . now," wheezed the dying man. "Find out . . . who's behind . . . this Ghost of Mystery Rancho, Roy. You an' me . . . know ghosts don't exist. Some flesh and blood . . . man behind this hoax—"

The old Ranger's voice trailed off in a rattle of final agony. A shudder went through the man's frame, and slowly his scrawny muscles relaxed, his eyes still holding their pleading gravity as they stared back at Roy Rogers.

Knowing his friend was dead, Roy Rogers whispered brokenly, "I'll tote your Ranger star until either the Ghost or me is dead, John. I pledge my word on that."

CHAPTER II

ESCAPING GUNMAN

Staring through the archway into the semi-gloom of the mission's interior, Roy Rogers felt a shock of surprise as he saw the seated skeleton facing him.

A wisp of powder smoke was curling from the rusty bore of the cap-and-ball Dragoon pistol resting on the skeleton's right knee. The other pistol was at full cock.

Half ashamed at his own reactions, Rogers side-stepped quickly to get his own body out of range of the two guns held in the skeleton's talon-like fingers.

Except for the fact that John Whetlaw lay dead outside this Haunted Mission, the cowboy would have believed that his imagination was playing him tricks. How could a moldy skeleton pull the trigger of a heavy six-gun to kill a human target? It was impossible, absurd. And yet it had happened.

Even as he peered around the corner of the adobe opening, Roy Rogers saw the skull's lower jaw move in a jerky fashion, like a ventriloquist's wooden dummy. A strange, hollow voice addressed him.

"Take the Ranger and ride, cowboy. The Ghost of Mystery Rancho allows no strangers inside Tomahawk Basin."

Rogers hefted his cocked six-guns, ashamed of the icy sweat which popped out on his forehead. Almost without willing to do so, the cowboy retorted, "Skeletons can't talk any more than they can shoot. We'll see if you can take lead as well as sling it."

The heavy Colts recoiled violently against the crotch of Roy's thumbs as he fired point-blank at the grinning skull.

Through clouding gunsmoke, Rogers saw his slugs strike the Talking Skull, saw that Stetson-clad death's-head roll off to hit the earthen floor of the chapel with a dull thud.

With his ears ringing from the blast of his own guns, Roy Rogers started to cross the wooden threshold where John Whetlaw had met his death. Some instinct of danger made him draw back out of range of the headless skeleton's leveled guns.

Acting on a hunch, Rogers reached out a boot-clad foot and gave the door's threshold timber a hard kick.

Instantly the skeleton's second pistol exploded, driving its bullet through space alongside Rogers.

In that instant, the cowboy knew he had solved the mystery of the Ranger captain's murder. Two parallel lines across the disturbed dust of the mission floor revealed where twin wires were stretched from the skeleton's chair to the threshold timber.

Knowing he was safe now, Rogers stepped inside,

his eyes quickly sizing up the musty interior of the ruined mission. He put his back to the adobe wall beside the door, where he would be difficult to see in the darkness.

Aside from the flutter of disturbed swallows up in the eaves, there was no sound inside this ancient structure, no hint of any menace lurking in the shadows. The Talking Skull, punched through with Rogers's two bullet holes, lay on the dusty floor.

As his eyes became accustomed to the dim light, the cowboy saw that the skeleton's chair had been placed against an interior wall of whitewashed adobe brick. And directly behind the spot where the Talking Skull had rested atop the skeleton's shoulders was a round hole, such as a rat might have made.

Protruding from that hole was a snakelike object which ended with a brass collar, the metal gleaming from the sunshine which shafted through the open doorway.

Stalking forward, guns ready for action at the slightest alien sound in this gloom, Roy Rogers took a close look at the strange brass-tipped object which protruded from the hole in the crumbling wall.

It was the end of an ordinary piece of garden hose!

Roy Rogers sucked in a deep breath. That garden hose held a morbid significance to him. It had served as a speaking tube—some human being had sent his voice into the other end of that hose!

Roy Held His Guns on the Skeleton

On second look, the rider saw a broken end of
twine protruding from the hole. That string, he
knew, had been connected to the Talking Skull's
jawbone. When it was jerked by human hands, it had
caused the jaw to move.

With a boot toe Rogers nudged one of the wires
which led from the threshold board. He saw now
where these wires led up the chair legs, held in place
with small staples, each wire having been connected
to the hair triggers of the cap-and-ball pistols in the
skeleton's hands.

Whoever put his weight on one side or the other
of the carefully balanced threshold would tighten
those wires sufficiently to trip the skeleton's gunhammers. In all his experience on the Western
frontier, Roy Rogers had never run across a more
fiendish or cunningly designed murder trap than
this one which had slain Ranger John Whetlaw.

Swiftly, Rogers stepped to an opening in the wall
behind the seated skeleton and passed through into
deeper darkness.

A shaft of sunlight slanting down from a break in
the Haunted Mission's roof revealed the black, ser-
pent-like line of the garden hose leading up that
wall's back surface, through a hole between two
rafters.

Groping his way toward a section of broken wall
leading to the outdoors, Rogers was in the act of

peering around the jagged edges of the mud bricks when a gunshot broke the haunted quiet.

A bullet struck the adobe wall an inch from his head, spraying his cheek with flying particles. The shot had come from high up—from the direction of the mission's bell tower.

Whoever had operated the Talking Skull had done so, then, from the tower. To expose himself in the open at this section of the mission would result in certain death.

Crouched low, Roy Rogers raced back through the mission, passed the headless skeleton and leaped through the doorway where John Whetlaw had met his doom.

At that instant one of the corroded bronze bells in the mission tower emitted a solemn, tolling note.

Running out from the mission wall, Rogers turned in time to learn the reason for that single resounding bell note.

A human figure was sliding down the rawhide bell rope, hitting the ground just as Rogers turned that way.

The cowboy whipped up his guns and laid two shots at the figure, but knew he had failed to hit the man's legs as the mysterious shape vanished around the corner of the building.

In that fleeting glimpse, only one identifying factor was left in Rogers's mind: the killer of John

Whetlaw wore a bright scarlet-colored rodeo shirt with crescent-shaped pockets.

Flanking the crumbling mission wall, Rogers reached the corner where the killer had vanished in time to hear the sharp strike of steel-shod hoofs hammering off down-slope beyond a thicket of chaparral which grew jungle-like to the very walls of Haunted Mission.

Shaking his head with disappointment, Rogers listened to the drumming of hoofbeats fade off, heading down the steep ridge into Tomahawk Basin.

Pursuit would be useless, he knew. A stranger here, Rogers had no way of knowing the killer's route through the webwork of game trails which threaded the chaparral. To follow the killer would be laying himself wide open to an ambush—and that would be a poor start toward fulfilling the pledge he had given the dying Ranger.

He walked around to the back of the bell tower and confirmed the fact that the length of garden hose led up the rear wall to vanish inside one of the bell-hung windows.

The killer, waiting for Whetlaw to show up at this place, had scaled a bell rope to reach the tower. From there he had addressed his ghostly words into the upper end of the hose, which accounted for the unearthly tone of the Talking Skull's voice. Like a marionette artist manipulating a puppet's wires, the killer had twitched the string which was tied to the skull's hinged jaw.

Thinking this thing out, Rogers came to one conclusion. Whetlaw had sent a telegram to Buck Conroy, telling him when to expect him at High Gate. Conroy had hidden a message under the Painted Rock at the smoke tree's roots, instructing the Ranger to meet him at the Haunted Mission.

"If Conroy's trying to save Mystery Rancho, why should he send for a Ranger and then murder him?" Rogers mumbled to himself, reloading his guns and thrusting them into holsters. "It doesn't make sense. But then, none of this Ghost business has made sense from the beginning."

One thing was clear. Whether or not Buck Conroy had lured John Whetlaw to his death, Roy Rogers would have to ride on down to Box C ranch and size up the Texas rancher first hand. To do otherwise would be admitting that he was afraid of the Talking Skull's blunt warning.

Returning to the front of the Haunted Mission, Rogers put his index fingers between his teeth and whistled. Instantly his highly trained palomino pricked up its ears and left the Spanish Trail, heading up the slope.

Whetlaw's horse, dragging its reins, hesitated a moment and then followed Trigger.

Taut-cheeked with the pressure of the personal

grief that rode him, Roy Rogers lifted the dead Ranger and tied him across his own saddle.

He hooked a stirrup over his own saddle horn, the silver trappings flashing in the sunlight. After tightening the latigo, Rogers mounted and leaned out to catch up the Ranger's trail rope.

The sun was still an hour above the jagged horizon, but Rogers saw no need now to wait for darkness before approaching Box C. The Ghost of Mystery Rancho—or one of his henchman—was already too well aware of Rogers's presence here.

Heading on down to pick up the Spanish Trail out of High Gate, Roy Rogers turned in the direction of the ranch buildings which lay on the hazy floor of Tomahawk Basin.

Somewhere down there a killer in a bright scarlet shirt had preceded him. He wondered what he would do if Buck Conroy turned out to be wearing a scarlet shirt when he met him at Mystery Rancho.

Common sense told Rogers that he might be heading directly into a murder trap on Box C, but that was a risk he would have to run. He had given a dying man his oath of honor to solve this uncanny riddle, and for Roy there was no other way out than to ride boldly to the headquarters of Mystery Rancho.

Grim-faced, Roy headed Trigger down the Spanish Trail.

CHAPTER III

THE SCARLET SHIRT

The first stars were glinting behind the burned-out glare of sunset when Roy Rogers swung out of stirrups in front of a rustic gate, the log arch of which had a set of elk horns nailed to its center with the Box C brand burned into the elk's skull.

Leaving Trigger groundhitched outside the neat picket fence which enclosed a smooth, green lawn, the young cowboy headed up a flower-bordered path toward the rambling adobe ranch house.

The red eye of a cigar coal ebbed and glowed in the darkness of the railed gallery flanking the front of the Conroy home. As Rogers reached the porch steps he heard a rocking chair cease its motion as its occupant stood up and stepped into a bar of lamplight shining through the open doorway.

"Howdy, stranger," came a deep Texas drawl from the tall, silver-haired oldster who stood there. Then, catching sight of the Texas Ranger badge glinting from Rogers's shirt, the old man sucked a breath under his white mustache and stepped forward, one bony hand extended. "Why, you're John

Whetlaw. How come you didn't wire me when you were arrivin', Captain?"

Over the handshake, Rogers was taking in the appearance of this massive-built old Texan, knowing he was Buck Conroy, owner of Mystery Rancho. Conroy was not wearing a scarlet shirt; his garb consisted of bullhide chaps which followed the bow of his saddle-warped legs, a spotted calfhide vest and a plain hickory shirt, blue and faded. A cedar-butted Colt sagged in its holster at Conroy's flank, pulling down the cartridge-studded gun belt.

"My name is Roy Rogers," the cowboy said. "Before I tell you why I came to Mystery Rancho in Whetlaw's place, I might mention that Whetlaw *did* telegraph you from San Antonio telling you we would reach High Gate today. Otherwise, how'd we know to pick up this message you left under the Painted Rock?"

As he spoke, Roy handed Conroy the note he had removed from Whetlaw's pocket. Staring at the paper, Conroy said, "I never saw this message before, Rogers. It's a forgery. I haven't heard a word from Ranger headquarters since I wired for help."

Rogers's ice-blue eyes narrowed puzzledly. "You didn't instruct Whetlaw to meet you at Haunted Mission?"

Conroy looked more puzzled than ever. "Haunted Mission? Why, I haven't visited those old ruins in fifteen years. Altitude is too much for my heart. As for High Gate—I had expected to meet Whetlaw at the stagecoach station in Gunsight."

In this moment, staring into Conroy's faded but eagle-keen eyes, Roy Rogers was convinced that the old man was telling the truth.

"Mr. Conroy," Rogers said slowly, "I've got bad news for you. That note there tricked Whetlaw into a murder trap up at the Haunted Mission late this afternoon. I've got his body out at your gate, tied to his own saddle."

Conroy swayed as if Rogers had struck him.

"The—the Ghost has struck again," he whispered. "Have you come to handle this case, Rogers? Knowin' it's a fifty-fifty bet you'll never leave Tomahawk Basin alive?"

Rogers shrugged. "I gave John my word," he said. "I've been a friend of Whetlaw's since I was a boy. With his dying breath he asked me to get to the bottom of this Mystery Rancho deal. With your help, sir, I intend to bring the so-called Ghost to justice. The Ghost is a human being, of course."

Apologizing for having kept his guest waiting outside, Conroy escorted the cowboy into his living-room, where a fire crackled in a huge rock hearth. This room was decorated in the Western style, with Navajo rugs and coyote skins on the floors, mounted heads of wild animals adorning the walls, and furniture **made** on the ranch of rawhide and native wood, horsehide and loblolly pine.

As he entered, removing his Stetson, Roy Rogers saw a lone man seated on a horsehide sofa in front of the fireplace. He was young and massively built, and he wore waist overalls and a plaid shirt. When this man turned at the sound of their approach, the play of firelight on his face revealed that his cheeks and forehead were horribly scarred, as if from a fire, and he wore a pair of dark green glasses.

"This is my ranch foreman, Jingo Bates," Conroy said. "This is Texas Ranger Roy Rogers, Jingo. He has come to crack this hoodoo which overhangs the Box C."

Jingo Bates stood up, groping a hand in Roy's direction. In that moment, Rogers realized that the Box C ramrod was totally blind, and a rush of pity went through him as he shook hands.

"You're loco, Rogers, to tackle this thing," rasped the blind foreman, his wide mouth twisting bitterly. "I hope you are luckier than I was. The Ghost destroyed my eyesight. I hope he kills you outright, swiftly and mercifully."

While Roy was trying to think of an adequate reply to this embittered outburst, Buck Conroy said gently, "Jingo, send a roustabout out to the front gate to take care of Roy's horse. And there'll be a dead man on the other horse out there—John Whetlaw, the Ranger. Have his body carried to the spare bunkhouse. And send a rider over to Gunsight to get the coroner."

Jingo Bates shrugged, turned on his heel and headed across the big room, moving with a sure-footed familiarity with his surroundings. When he had disappeared through a doorway, Conroy waved Roy Rogers into the sofa Jingo Bates had just vacated. Lifting his voice, the Box C boss summoned a Chinese servant from a remote part of the house.

"Fung Ling, we have a guest. Prepare him a supper pronto. I reckon he's hungry enough to eat a wolf."

When the moon-faced Chinese had departed, Conroy sat down beside Roy Rogers.

"Tell me, Mr. Conroy—what is this Mystery Rancho hoodoo?"

Conroy laced his gnarled fingers together over an uplifted knee, staring moodily into the dancing flames, his face shadowed with tragic memories.

"The Ghost of Mystery Rancho," Conroy said finally, "is a rider who is apparently bulletproof. Heaven knows enough of us have slung lead at him in the past few months. He wears a mask which resembles a skull, with grinning teeth and hollow eye sockets. His costume is a fantastic one which glows at night, making him seem like an animated skeleton. Those who have seen the Ghost in full daylight say his shirt is black, painted with white stripes like ribs and vertebrae. His chaps are black with leg and hip bones either painted on them or inlaid with white leather."

Roy Rogers considered this information gravely.

"The Ghost first struck," Conroy went on in a heavy voice, "some fifteen months ago. My foreman, Jingo Bates, was repairing our drift fence which is built along the international boundary line between Texas and Mexico, on the banks of the Rio Grande."

Conroy shuddered at the memory.

"This skull-masked Ghost appeared on the Mexican side of the Rio and swam his horse over to where Jingo was waiting. He offered Jingo a fat bribe— five thousand in 'dobe dollars—to try and ambush me. When Jingo refused, the Ghost drew a bottle of soft pitch from his saddlebags, lighted it, and hurled that flaming mass in Jingo's face. When Jingo got to a doctor over in Gunsight, it was too late to save him from lifelong blindness."

Fung Ling, the cook, announced in his singsong voice that supper was ready in the dining-room, and Conroy did not resume his narrative until Roy Rogers was busy putting away the first square meal he had had in forty-eight hours.

"I've kept Jingo on the payroll through a feeling of gratitude toward him," Conroy said. "But the Ghost has murdered some of my line riders. He has set fire to my graze, poisoned my best water holes, driven my superstitious Mexican *vaqueros* off the ranch. I'm almost bankrupt, Roy. Box C can't hire riders any more. Only when my back was to the wall did I decide to call for help from the Texas Rangers."

Roy stirred sugar into his third cup of coffee. "And you have no idea," he said, "who the Ghost might be, or what his motive is for wanting to drive you off the ranch?"

Conroy ran spread fingers through his mane of silvery hair.

"No to both questions, Roy. I believe the Ghost may be a Mexican—perhaps the notorious smuggler king from Chihuahua, the outlaw the Mexican *rurale* police call Señor Rattlesnake. As a guess, I would say that Señor Rattlesnake wants to possess Mystery Rancho—as the Mexicans now call Box C —because it lies so handy to the border, and would therefore be ideal for Señor Rattlesnake's smuggling operations. But that is only a guess—which is shared, by the way, by the Border Patrol, the United States Customs, and the federal marshals who have tried to crack this case. That isn't much to go on, but—"

Conroy was interrupted by the arrival of a surly-faced *mestizo*. A ball-tassled sombrero was tipped back on the man's head and his eyes reminded Roy Rogers of a snake's as he turned to Buck Conroy.

"I have taken care of the horses, Don Buck, and have taken thos' dead man to the bunkhouse. Ees it all right for me to go now?"

Conroy nodded. "I'm sorry I interrupted your amusement for such a trivial thing, Bronc," the rancher said ironically.

After the surly man had left, Conroy said, "That was my cavvy wrangler, Bronc Alamar. You can see how discipline has gone down, Roy. What few men I can get to work for me are insolent and lazy, downright insulting and disobedient. Bronc Alamar is their ringleader. If Jingo had his eyesight, the first thing he would do would be to thrash Alamar soundly—and then fire him."

Finishing his supper, Roy followed Conroy back to the front room. They found Jingo Bates seated once more at the fireplace, the light shimmering off his dark glasses, his face wearing an expression of utter listlessness.

"Jingo," Conroy said anxiously, "have you any idea where Texanna is? She shouldn't be out this time of night."

Bates shrugged. "Your daughter seems to enjoy moonlight canters," the blind foreman said bleakly. "All I know is that she's been gone with her pony since the middle of the afternoon. Maybe she went over to Gunsight to visit her friend the sheriff, Tommy Stockton."

They Talked to the Blind Foreman

Roy saw Conroy flush with embarrassment, and he detected a strong note of jealousy in Bates's voice as he mentioned the name of the girl's friend in Gunsight. Before his tragedy at the hands of the vicious Ghost, Roy imagined that Jingo Bates had had romantic designs on the rancher's daughter.

Into the run of awkward silence which followed Bates's words, there came a jingle of spur chains on the porch outside. The door swung open and into the firelight strode a tall, willowy girl in her late teens, wearing a split buckskin skirt, taffy-colored boots—and a *bright scarlet shirt with white crescent-shaped pockets.*

Roy Rogers felt his heart slam his ribs as he saw the girl remove her cream-colored Stetson, scale it through space to hang it on a deerhorn rack on a far wall, and then, shaking back her long auburn tresses, cross the room to plant a kiss on old Buck Conroy's cheek.

"Worried about me, Daddy?" The girl laughed. "I just had the pinto shod and I was trying him out. I—oh, excuse me. I didn't know—you had visitors."

Conroy turned to Roy Rogers, sliding an arm around the young woman's waist.

"My daughter, Texanna. Tex, this is Roy Rogers, a Texas Ranger who has come from San Antone to investigate this mystery for us."

Roy found himself at a loss for words as he met

Texanna Conroy's smiling amber eyes, accepted her hand and found her grip as strong as a man's. Was it possible that this beautiful cowgirl was the slayer of John Whetlaw? Had she been the mystery voice behind the Talking Skull out at Haunted Mission this afternoon? Her shirt was identical to the one Rogers had seen on the vanishing gunman who had slid down the bell-rope from the mission tower.

"Welcome to Box C, Roy," Texanna said. "Hello, Jingo. Has Fung Ling saved me something to eat?"

Rogers grinned crookedly. "That's a right perty shirt you're wearin', Miss Conroy."

Texanna glanced down at the vivid scarlet garment.

"Oh, this red horror? It's a throwback to the days when Box C used to take part in the annual rodeo over at Gunsight. It's our ranch uniform, you might say. Every Box C rider wore one of these scarlet shirts. The crescent trim on the square pockets is supposed to represent our brand, the Box C."

With that Texanna excused herself and headed for the kitchen to wangle a meal from the Chinese cook. Had Roy imagined that she had cast him a challenging, taunting look while she had explained the origin of her scarlet shirt? At any rate, she had said enough to tell Roy Rogers that Whetlaw's murderer could have been any former waddy on the Box C owning such an identical garment.

CHAPTER IV

BULLETPROOF GHOST

Declining Conroy's invitation to sleep in the main house, Roy made his way out to the Box C bunkhouse. By making his living quarters there, the cowboy believed he would be better able to study the men who worked for Conroy, size up their loyalties and, if possible, glean some clue as to the Ghost's depredations.

Even as he pushed open the door of the bunkhouse, he saw that he had arrived to witness the climax of a brutal scene.

The fat Chinese cook, Fung Ling, was down on his knees on the puncheon floor, struggling to release himself from the strangling noose of his own queue.

His attacker was the surly cavvy wrangler, Bronc Alamar, who had put a dally of the cook's black hair around his throat and was slowly choking the unfortunate man into insensibility.

Off to one side, three grinning waddies were seated at a table, watching the husky wrangler punish Fung Ling.

Unable to endure the cook's agonized, strangled cries, Roy Rogers strode across the floor and seized

Alamar by the arm, breaking his grip.

As the Chinese fell moaning to the floor, Alamar whirled, snarling like a wolf at bay. Recognizing Roy Rogers, Bronc Alamar stabbed a hand to gun-butt and jerked his long-barreled .45 into the open.

Moving with incredible speed, Roy Rogers kicked the gun from the wrangler's fist and followed it with a looping haymaker which struck Alamar's stubbly jaw with a resounding meaty impact.

Knocked staggering by Rogers's heavy blow, Alamar brought up against the bunkhouse stove, knocking the smoke pipe apart and bringing a cascade of soot over his head and shoulders.

Before Alamar could shake the daze out of his brain and draw his second gun, he found himself staring into the black muzzle of Roy Rogers's ivory-handled Colt.

"What is this?" Roy demanded. "What's the trouble?"

Alamar, too dazed and angry to reply, stood rubbing his bloody jaw. Fung Ling had crawled over to a bunk and stretched out on it, massaging his bruised throat, his oblique almond eyes flashing their message of gratitude to Roy Rogers.

One of the cowboys spoke up respectfully. "Put yore gun away, kid. Alamar didn't mean nothin'. He just hates all Chinese. That's why he makes life miserable for the cookee yonder."

Roy's lips curled with disgust as he holstered his gun.

"I feel sorry for any man who hates another human just because of his religion or the color of his skin," Rogers said contemptuously.

"I get even for this," warned the wrangler.

Rogers went directly to the bunk Conroy had assigned him and slowly started shucking off his cowboots. He regretted this poor start to his residence on Mystery Rancho; he knew that in Bronc Alamar he had made a deadly foe, one who might not be above attempting to knife him in the back if the opportunity presented itself.

But he knew, too, that he had gained the respect, perhaps the admiration of the three other cowboys in this bunkhouse by his manhandling of the bully in their midst. It was obvious from Alamar's defiant attitude to the others that they hated and feared him.

Next morning, it was the jangling of Fung Ling's triangle at the cookhouse which roused Roy Rogers from a sound sleep. Swinging out of the blankets, the newcomer saw that his twin six-guns and shell belts were lying on the floor by his bunk instead of hanging on the peg where he had left them.

A puzzled frown carved its notch between Roy's brows as he started dressing. Had someone tampered with his guns during the night, while he slept the sleep of exhaustion from his long trek into the Big Bend? It seemed improbable that the heavy weapons could have dropped off the peg by themselves.

The blind foreman, Jingo Bates, occupied the bunk next to him; the one overhead was occupied by Bronc Alamar. Either man could have reached his gun harness without leaving his bed.

While the others were outside washing and shaving, Roy took the trouble to make sure his .45's were loaded and the cylinders in complete working order. He checked the rifled bores for possible obstructions, but found none.

He thought to himself, *My nerves must be getting jumpy,* and dismissed the matter from his mind.

Immediately after breakfast, Roy Rogers went out to the cavvy corral and threw his silver-mounted saddle on Trigger.

Then he headed away from the Box C ranch, riding south across the level floor of Tomahawk Basin in the direction of the Rio Grande. His purpose for this early-morning ride was to acquaint himself with his surroundings, size up the lay of the land.

Approaching the Rio Grande, Roy found vast acreages of burned-over land, the bunch grass and sage dead and blackened. He remembered what Buck Conroy had told him last night about the Mystery Rancho Ghost's setting prairie fires in order to destroy Box C's graze.

He came finally to the drift fence which followed the curves of the Rio Grande's north bank. It was along this fence somewhere that Jingo Bates had been mutilated by the Ghost.

Letting Trigger graze, Roy stared off across the muddy yellow waters of the sluggish-flowing Rio, contemplating the rough, broken badlands on the Chihuahua side. Over there was the lawless domain of the smuggler king, Señor Rattlesnake. Somewhere in those creased, arid mountain uplands might be the key to the mystery of the Ghost and all his evil works.

Hipping around in saddle, Roy trained his eye on the north skyline, locating the notch of High Gate and seeing the ruins of Haunted Mission etched against the enamel-blue sky.

While thus engaged he heard a drumming of hoofs and swung around to see Texanna Conroy approaching from the direction of the ranch, riding a close-coupled paint pony.

The girl was still wearing her scarlet shirt, making a bright contrast to the drab background of the Basin. She was laughing as she reined up alongside Roy's stirrup, her face aglow with vitality.

"Mind if I join you?" she said. "You're sizing up the ranch, aren't you? Maybe I could show you a few landmarks, Roy."

Rogers grinned in spite of himself. He would have

preferred to work alone this morning, but it was difficult to refuse this charming young woman.

"Sure Tommy Stockton won't object?" he said teasingly.

Texanna's face clouded briefly.

"Jingo Bates must have told you about Tommy," she said. "Tommy is sheriff over at Gunsight—that's the only town in this part of the Big Bend. It's a mining camp, really—over in a canyon in the Navajadas yonder. I—I sort of go with Tommy Stockton."

Roy grinned. "Tommy's a lucky man. Jingo Bates doesn't approve of the match, I take it?"

Texanna smiled ruefully. "Poor Jingo—before he was blinded, he used to take me to dances over in Gunsight. I—I think he was falling in love with me. But I never felt that way about Jingo—even before his misfortune. So—"

Texanna Conroy broke off as she saw Roy Rogers suddenly stiffen in saddle, his lean, rope-calloused hands flashing to his thighs. Sunlight flashed off the blued surfaces of his six-guns as Rogers made his double draw, so rapidly that the girl's eyes could not follow his move.

Roy was staring off past the girl, toward the brushy mouth of a draw some fifty feet away.

Wheeling her horse, Texanna gave a low scream at what she saw. Standing just outside the cactus thickets at the entrance of the defile was a tall figure in a skeleton-designed costume, his head resembling a human skull.

"It—it's the Ghost!" Texanna's low voice reached Roy Rogers's ears. "Oh, Roy—I'm afraid—"

Trigger moved forward to put Rogers between the girl and the Ghost of Mystery Rancho. So far, the spooky figure had not moved, standing so stock-still he resembled a statue.

Thumbs holding his Colts at full cock, Roy Rogers put Trigger forward in a beeline toward the motionless apparition in the skeleton costume. The palomino halted instantly when the Mystery Rancho Ghost's gloved hands dropped suddenly to the bright red butts of low-slung, thonged-down six-guns.

Expecting gunplay to break here at any instant, Roy yelled, "Ride out of the line of fire, Texanna—"

He heard a throaty laugh issue from behind the Ghost's skull mask, as Texanna spurred her pinto closer to the Rio Grande drift fence.

Speaking in rapid Spanish—a language Roy Rogers understood as readily as his own tongue—the Ghost said, "I'm giving you twenty-four hours to leave the Basin, Señor Rogers. Otherwise they'll be burying you alongside El Capitan Whetlaw—"

Roy Rogers lifted his guns, taking a cool and deliberate aim on the Ghost's big frame.

"Get your arms up, Ghost!" he shouted in Spanish.

"*Maños altos!* I'm arresting you in the name of the State of Texas—"

With a jeering laugh, the Mystery Rancho Ghost turned his back to Roy Rogers and, crouching, headed into the cactus-choked mouth of the draw.

Unwilling to shoot even this craven outlaw in the back, Rogers notched his gunsights on the fleeing Ghost's legs and dropped gunhammers.

The heavy roar of the guns was flung back in tangled echoes from the Mexican side of the river. But as the powder smoke cleared in the sultry air, Roy Rogers did not see the sprawled, writhing shape of a crippled target at the mouth of the defile.

The Ghost had vanished. And from the narrow mouth of the draw came the sound of his boots slogging through rubble, the crash of brush as the Ghost made his swift retreat into the narrow gulch.

Unable to believe his eyes, Roy Rogers put Trigger into the defile, ignoring Texanna's scream of warning. A crack shot, it seemed impossible that he could have missed both shots completely, at such close range. And he knew that no bulletproof pants had been invented which could stop the impact of heavy-calibered .45 bullets.

Before he had bucked the thorny jungle twenty feet, Roy realized it was impossible for a horse to penetrate it. Even a man would have to crawl on his stomach to manage a getaway along this arroyo.

He heard Texanna screaming his name just as he was thinking of leaving Trigger here and following the Ghost's tracks into the cactus thickets. Now, fearing the girl might be in danger, Roy swung the palomino around and returned to the mouth of the draw.

The girl was still on her horse, unhurt. She was pointing off across the Rio Grande.

Looking in that direction, Rogers was amazed to see the skeleton-suited Ghost, mounted now on a black stallion, on the river bank on the Mexican side of the Rio!

It seemed impossible that the Ghost could have spanned that hundred-yard barrier of muddy water. Safely out of range of Roy's guns, the Ghost waved derisively, wheeled his horse, and vanished behind a pile of boulders.

"The superstitious peons around here think that the Ghost's horse has winged feet," Texanna said, understanding Roy's bewilderment. "You'd almost think he flew to the Mexico side, at that."

Rogers tore his gaze from the rocks where the Ghost had disappeared, knowing that he and Texanna were prime targets for a .30-30 Winchester at this range.

Ordering Texanna to follow him, Roy put a jut of ground between him and the Chihuahua boulder nest. His smoking Colts were still in his hands, and while the girl watched, Roy holstered one of the guns and jacked open the cylinder of the other to spill the cartridges out into his palm.

"One thing is certain," the girl said, "the Ghost is actually bulletproof. At point-blank range, your guns were useless—"

Upon close inspection, Roy made a dismaying discovery. The lead slugs in his shells were not solid bullets—they were clever imitations formed of lead foil! Squeezed between thumb and forefinger, the bullets flattened out like paper!

"No, Texanna," Roy said grimly. "The Ghost isn't bulletproof. Someone unloaded my guns in the bunkhouse last night and substituted cartridges with imitation dummy loads. No wonder the Ghost escaped just now."

Texanna's eyes widened with horror. "Then—that means the Ghost has an accomplice in Dad's very crew!" the girl cried. "Oh, Roy—you and I must make Dad sell Box C before we're all killed. You've had your warning from the Ghost—you won't get another one."

Rogers looked up at the girl while he reloaded his guns with genuine cartridges from his belt loops.

"Texanna," he said, "I want you to ride back home at once. I'm going to solve the mystery of how the Ghost 'flew' across the Rio Grande, and I'm going to start now."

CHAPTER V

QUICKSAND DOOM!

After some argument, Texanna Conroy spurred her pinto into a gallop and lined off across the Basin in the direction of her father's ranch.

When she was out of sight, Roy Rogers sent Trigger up the steep shoulder on the south side of the cactus-choked defile where the Ghost had disappeared, and followed its rimrock for fifty yards.

The far end of the draw ended on a slope leading up to a bench of level ground where Trigger now stood. The Ghost's footprints were plainly visible in the crumbled adobe dust. They led to a spot a few yards away where a horse—no doubt the black stallion—had been waiting.

Spurring Trigger forward, Roy followed the tracks, knowing they would have to veer right or left eventually in order to avoid the sheer flank of the butte.

A moment later he heard Trigger snort with panic as the palomino's forehoofs broke through the sandy crust of the ground and instantly sank to the fetlock joints.

Trigger lunged back on his hind hoofs and reared

aloft, his forehoofs breaking free of the soft sands with an odd sucking noise. Not even the touch of Rogers's star-roweled spurs—worn more for ornament than use—could make the trembling palomino approach the broken crust of sand again.

"What's wrong, Trigger boy?" Rogers said anxiously. The horse blew through its nostrils and flung its head from side to side, plainly indicating that danger lurked under those innocent-appearing sands.

Scowling, Roy swung out of saddle and cautiously approached the twin depressions where Trigger's hoofs had broken through. They were rapidly leveling off as soft sand poured into them.

On a hunch, Roy picked up a brick-sized gabbro rock and tossed it a dozen feet ahead of him. The rock broke through the surface crust of gray sand. Before his eyes, the rock settled out of sight, leaving only a dimple in the sand.

"I get it, Trigger," Roy whispered. "This is a *sumidero*—a quicksand bog. And yet the Ghost's horse headed right into that patch of quicksand."

It was true. The faint outlines of the Ghost's mount were clearly visible. They stopped abruptly at the edge of the area of solid ground which rimmed the quicksand *sumidero*.

"Off-hand, I'd say that the Ghost and his horse were sucked under the surface of that quicksand."

Roy spoke to Trigger, a habit which he had cultivated during the time he and the palomino had traveled the adventure trails of the West. "But we saw the Ghost on the Mexico side of the Rio—"

Squatting there on the very brink of the quicksand bog, Roy lifted his eyes to stare at the base of the sheer granite wall which formed the opposite limits of the *sumidero.*

A heavy growth of flowering desert shrubs furred the base of the low cliff, indicating solid earth at that point. Projecting above the bushes was the whitened snag of a dead smoke tree.

For long moments, Roy pondered what to do next. The Ghost had obviously had some way of crossing this quicksand area—but how? And once he had reached the base of the butte, by what manner had he breached that solid barrier of stone?

Stepping over to where Trigger waited hip-shot on three feet, still quivering from his narrow escape from the deadly sands, Roy Rogers unbuckled the coil of lariat from his pommel.

Shaking out a loop with a cowboy's deft hand, Roy got his lasso whirling overhead and made his cast, sending the lariat snaking out across the quicksand bog to drop its wide loop over the smoke tree snag.

Pulling the rope taut, Roy tested the snag's strength by putting all his weight on the rope. Convinced that the smoke tree would support his own bulk, Roy dallied the other end of the riata over his saddle horn.

Trigger needed no order to step back, bringing the rope taut as a fiddle string, at a height of about five feet above the menace of the quicksand bog.

"Just hold her there, Trigger, and make sure you keep up the slack," Rogers said. "I'm going to cross that *sumidero* and see if I can cut the Ghost's sign on the far side."

Trigger snorted nervously as Roy Rogers got a grip on the rope with both hands. Automatically the palomino backed off another step to pull the rope level again under the weight of his rider.

Pulling up his knees, Rogers started out over the *sumidero,* working his cautious way hand-over-hand along the taut rope. His shadow waggled over the smooth sandy crust of the quicksand, his boots inches above those waiting, deadly depths.

The *sumidero* was some twenty feet across. When Roy had reached the halfway point, his ears caught the jarring sound of human laughter issuing from the dense brush ahead of him.

Horror laid its icy fingers on the cowboy's heart as he realized his own helpless position. To drop to the ground and draw his guns would mean certain death in the waiting quicksand below; to wait here, hanging by both arms from the rope, would make him a perfect target for whatever gunman lurked behind those tangled bushes. And that gunman might be the Ghost himself!

A moment later Roy saw the brush shake immediately below the smoke tree snag where his lasso was anchored.

Sunlight flashed on naked steel behind the foliage there. The brush was too thick for Roy to make out the figure he knew was crouching alongside the trunk of the smoke tree snag.

Then, while Rogers hung motionless over the *sumidero*, he saw a brown-skinned, hairy arm reach up above the brush toward the rope. That hand clutched a long-bladed Mexican *cuchillo* or bowie knife.

. In the agonizing seconds that it took the hidden outlaw to reach the taut-stretched rope with his knife blade, Roy's eyes detected something else.

Tattooed in blue ink around that hairy brown arm, from wrist to elbow, was the likeness of a coiled rattlesnake.

The first touch of the razor-honed knife blade on the rope transmitted itself to Roy Rogers's fists.

An instant later the rope parted, neatly cut an inch from the brass honda of the lariat.

As the rope flew back, Roy felt himself dropping to his knees, his weight breaking through the quicksand bog's crust instantly.

Roy Was Directly Over the Quicksand

Flinging the useless rope aside, Roy jerked his guns from holsters as he saw the brush moving violently.

His guns blazed deafeningly, bullets clipping through the brambles where the rattlesnake-branded man was scuttling to safety.

Not knowing whether he had tallied his target or not, Roy Rogers holstered his guns and grabbed the slack lariat. In attempting to twist his body around to face his horse, Roy discovered that the quicksand was already up to his hips, the impact of his drop having wedged him deep under the shallow, fragile crust.

Wrapping several turns of the rope around his forearms, Roy yelled desperately, "All right, Trigger boy—pull! Pull!"

The palomino started backing away, sensing the fact that his master's life depended on his pulling Roy out of the sucking sands. Even as the rope went taut, putting a painful pressure on his arms, Roy knew this would be no easy escape.

Before Trigger's steady pull, it seemed to Roy that his arms would be wrenched out at the sockets. But slowly, ever so slowly, he felt his buried thighs begin to pull free of the greedy, death-dealing sands.

At that instant a gunshot broke the silence, coming from the heart of the brush at the foot of the cliff.

A bullet streaked its unseen path over Roy's

head—and he felt the lariat go slack in his hands, as the slug cut the wire-taut rope in two.

Trigger lunged back on his haunches as the rope let go.

Horror put its bitter taste in Roy Rogers's mouth as he realized what the rattlesnake-branded hombre had done. It had taken a dead shot to clip that rope as he had done, and in so doing, the outlaw had robbed the cowboy of his last hope of being tugged out of the *sumidero* alive.

Roy reached again for his guns, realizing then that the bores of those .45's were clogged with quicksand now, his open-toed holsters having sunk into the bog several inches. To fire the Colts now would make them explode in his hands, inflicting ruinous injury to his fingers.

Twisting his head in the direction of the brush, Roy half expected to see his foe's rifle barrel jutting into the open, aimed at his head.

Instead, he heard a sound of mysterious activity behind that hedge of thorns—a rattle of chains, a squeaking sound like a pair of heavy hinges turning.

Then came a heavy, sodden thud—the unmistakable sound of a huge door closing somewhere at the base of the granite cliff. After that there was only silence—the silence of death.

With a groan Roy Rogers loosened the buckles of his shell belts and hoisted them to armpit level before tightening them across his chest.

He knew, now, the fate that was in store for him. Instead of putting a merciful bullet through his brain, the rattlesnake-branded knifeman preferred to let him endure the agony of settling inch by inch into this *sumidero*.

Over at the edge of the quicksand bog, Trigger was pacing nervously back and forth, pawing the crust with a forehoof, as if trying to get up courage to come to his master's side.

"No, Trigger—stay back," panted Roy Rogers, feeling the deadly sands pouring down his bootlegs. "No use both of us dying in this trap."

Roy knew the futility of struggle. That would only make him sink faster. He was already hip-deep in the deadly ooze; at this rate he knew that his mouth and then his nostrils would be under the sucking sands before an hour had elapsed.

Flies swarmed around his head. The sun beat down with a punishing intensity, wetting the shirt to his back with its drawn-out moisture. His legs felt as if they were locked in vises. He was as solidly trapped as if he were in concrete.

There was no use shouting for help; this spot was a good five miles from Buck Conroy's ranch, and during his morning ride Roy had seen no one abroad on the Basin floor except Texanna Conroy. And he had sent the girl home for her own protection.

CHAPTER VI

In times of stress, Roy Rogers's alert brain always functioned at top efficiency.

Thumbing a soft-nose .45 bullet from his tooled-leather belts, Roy rummaged in a shirt pocket for a scrap of paper. On it, using the bullet for a pencil, the cowboy wrote:

Am in quicksand, far end of draw where Ghost vanished. Need help quickly.

Roy Rogers

Removing his cleft-crown Stetson, Roy thrust the folded paper inside the leather band.

Then, drawing back his arm, Roy sent the ten-gallon hat kiting through space, to land in a puff of dust alongside his pacing palomino.

"Take it home, Trigger—and fast!" Roy shouted.

Trigger circled his master's hat twice before reaching down his muzzle and gripping the brim between his teeth. Then the palomino flung his head up, staring at his doomed owner.

"Home, Trigger—home!"

The palomino flung his flaxen-maned neck toward the sky, swung around and, with the keen intelligence which Rogers's careful training had taken ad-

61

vantage of, broke into a full gallop, heading northeast in the direction of Box C.

To Trigger, "home" meant the last manger where he had been fed his oats, and that was Conroy's ranch.

A grin broke the taut corners of Roy's mouth as he saw Trigger increase speed and vanish beyond the roll of ground. The rapid beat of the palomino's hoofs faded on the sweltering air, and Roy Rogers knew that he had only one chance in a hundred of surviving until the horse could put his message into friendly hands.

From now on he had to play a waiting role. He tried to straighten his bent knees, but found that impossible. He regretted now that he was not at his full height; it was faintly possible that this quicksand bog was a shallow one, with a bedrock bottom on which his feet could lodge before the encroaching sands swallowed his head.

The Texas sun beating down added to his discomfort, and Roy removed his bandanna neckerchief and knotted it over his skull to give partial relief from the sun's blistering rays.

He realized that the weight of his guns added to the rate at which he was sinking. Each Peacemaker Colt scaled almost three pounds unloaded and besides there was the weight of his cartridge belts.

Reluctantly—because he still entertained the hope

that the outlaw who had dumped him into the quicksand might show up at any moment to gloat over his victim's predicament—Roy Rogers unbuckled his shell belts and, coiling them up, hurled them across the quicksand bog to land on solid ground. Now he was completely defenseless.

He thrust a hand under the quicksand and salvaged his pocket watch, finding it still running. He checked the time, assuming that he had been in the sand for about ten minutes, and tried to plot how long it would take the quicksand to reach above his nostrils.

As the minutes dragged by, each an eternity, Roy judged that he was going down at the rate of about an inch every ten minutes.

Later, when the level of the sand was above his throbbing heart, fast approaching his armpits, Roy realized that as he sank deeper, his rate of drop was increasing in speed as his lower body plunged into softer sand below the surface.

He heard no sound from the direction of the mysterious door in the base of the cliff. That door, he surmised, opened on a tunnel of some sort which probably crossed under the Rio Grande and came out on the Mexican side.

This tunnel would account for the Ghost of Mystery Rancho appearing, as if by magic, on the Chihuahua bank. But how had the Ghost and his horse safely crossed the *sumidero* to reach that door?

The sand crept up, up, up, reaching his armpits. He tried to support his weight with his arms on the *sumidero's* surface crust, but that was impossible; his elbows broke through immediately.

He was now forced to keep his arms in an elevated position, and the strain of that became well-nigh unendurable as time dragged by at a snail's pace.

He felt the sucking ooze of the bog trickle inch by inch over his shoulders. Breathing became increasingly difficult. Roy had never realized before that quicksand did not allow a man's lungs to expand and contract properly; the weight of the mire pressed in about his torso with increasing pressure, so that he could get air into his lungs only in short gasps.

Sweat blinded his eyes. His ears were humming loudly as his heart beat became more labored.

The sand crept up to his under jaw, started inching up his cheeks by slow degrees. Only his head and arms were above the deadly sands now. The watch in his shirt pocket was forever out of reach; he had no way of telling the passage of time.

High overhead in the Texas sky, a couple of black buzzards had spotted his plight and were spiraling lower and lower toward his trapped position.

He saw a diamondback rattlesnake gliding over the surface of the *sumidero,* a few feet away, its scaly length too spread out to break the crust.

Roy shouted frantically to divert the deadly reptile, heard the echo of his voice resound from the butte at his back.

It was his last chance to make a noise; the quicksand lifted above his mouth now. Another inch and the sands would cover his nostrils, and that would be the end.

Roy closed his eyes, almost praying for this thing to be finished, to bring relief from this unthinkable mental torture.

And then, above the drumming of blood in his ears, Roy Rogers thought he heard human voices shouting his name.

He opened his eyes—to see a pair of riders dismounting on the outer rim of the quicksand bog. Trigger was with them.

They were Jingo Bates on a grulla cow pony, and Texanna Conroy. Trigger had overtaken the girl in time and had brought help with mere seconds to spare!

While the blind Box C foreman held their reins, Texanna uncoiled her lariat with feverish haste and got her loop swirling with a cowgirl's deft skill.

"Roy! Roy—you'll have to grab this rope—can you hear me?"

Roy waved his hands in answer to her question.

Texanna's rope swished through space and the noose dropped expertly within reach of Roy's arms.

Roy pulled in what breath he could just as the sands reached his nose. Frantically he got his fists locked tightly around the noose, felt the girl draw in the slack.

"This is going to be a slow and painful job, Roy!" he heard Texanna's matter-of-fact voice. "We mustn't pull too hard or we'd break your spine."

Texanna and the blind ramrod put their combined weight on the rope and before the air had gone dead in Roy's lungs, his nose and mouth had been tugged clear of the strangling sands.

Exhaling, his face purple from holding his breath, Roy managed to gasp out, "Good . . . girl, Texanna. Better dally . . . your rope . . . around Trigger's . . . saddle horn. Let him . . . do the work . . ."

The girl hastened to carry out Roy's orders. Jingo Bates, the sun flashing on his green spectacles, stared across the quagmire with a blind man's impatience at missing this drama.

"Trigger caught up with me two miles out," Texanna said. "Luckily I was just jogging along, and I stopped when I saw your horse coming my way with an empty saddle."

A groan escaped Roy's locked teeth. Trigger's pull on the rope was a constant thing, but it threatened to pull his arms loose at the joints. Texanna, realizing what an ordeal Roy was enduring, halted Trigger and let the rope go slack for a moment's rest.

"Roy, Grab This Rope!"

"Trigger almost talked when he put your Stetson in my hands," the girl went on. "Just as I was reading your note, I saw Jingo out taking his usual morning ride. He joined me and we burned up the earth following Trigger back here."

The palomino resumed pulling and after an agonizing interval Roy Rogers's shoulders heaved up above the gurgling black sands. It was almost as if the *sumidero* was protesting the loss of its victim.

"You've had your share o' luck, Rogers," Jingo Bates said in his surly tone. "Take my advice, Ranger, and don't buck the Ghost again. You're lucky he didn't put your eyes out, the way he did to me. It's a grim thing, knowing you're in the dark the rest of your life."

It took an hour for Trigger to tug Rogers's torso out of the gripping sands. Roy knew he would have sore muscles and aching bones for weeks to come as a result of this ordeal. But physical discomfort was as nothing, compared to the new lease on life which was his. His thanks went out for the good work of his trained pony. More than once in the past, Trigger's intelligence had given Roy a new lease on life, but never before had the palomino rescued him from such a desperate plight as this.

"Better keep your eye—on the brush behind me, Texanna," he warned, when his hips were finally clear of the quicksand. "The Ghost might come back and start shooting. I—I wouldn't want you and Jingo to tangle with him on my behalf."

This news had a striking effect on Bates. With a mumbled word of apology to the girl, the blind man mounted his grulla and rode off out of sight.

"Can't blame Jingo for vamoosing," Texanna said. "After all, in case of trouble he couldn't do a thing. Oh, Roy—I hope this will be a lesson to you. I hope you'll leave Box C and never come back. This land has a curse on it."

A glint of high good humor came into Roy Rogers's eyes.

"I can never leave now," he said, "without getting my revenge on the Ghost. And likewise on an hombre with a rattlesnake tattooed on his arm. It was he who cut my rope and dropped me into this bog."

Texanna, waiting tensely on the firm ground by the *sumidero's* rim, turned a shade paler at what Roy said.

"A tattooed rattlesnake? Why, that's the notorious Mexican smuggler, Señor Rattlesnake. The Border Patrol's reward posters mention that tattooed snake in their description of him. Roy, this proves that Señor Rattlesnake and the Ghost are one and the same!"

Roy felt the clinging sands pull off his cowboots just as Trigger's steady pulling tugged his legs out of the mire.

When his body was free at last, Trigger had no difficulty in dragging Roy Rogers across the sandy crust, and he fell exhausted at Texanna's feet.

His first move was to ask for his guns. During one of the rest periods, Texanna had carefully cleaned out the bores, and the cowboy lost no time in buckling his gun harness back in place.

Texanna gave him a drink from her canteen. She put his sombrero, which still bore Trigger's tooth marks on the brim, on his sweat-plastered head and used the remainder of water in the canteen to wash the drying sand off his cheeks and neck.

Standing up, his legs wobbly from his ordeal, Roy stared down ruefully at his sock-clad feet. From his neck down, the cowboy was plastered with clinging mud.

"I'm tuckered out," he said. "I need a week of sleep, I reckon."

Roy swung his glance toward the base of the butte and the mysterious doorway it concealed. He knew he would never rest until he had solved the riddle of that doorway, for when he did that he would have his first tangible clue to the haunts of the Ghost of Mystery Rancho.

"Come on, Texanna," he said, pausing to pet Trigger's velvety muzzle. "We're riding. It's too dangerous here."

CHAPTER VII

SMUGGLERS' CAVE

Jingo Bates sat his horse a hundred yards out on the Basin floor as Roy and Texanna topped the hogback overlooking the river. Because he had a question which he did not want overheard to ask the girl, Roy pulled Trigger to a walk.

"Texanna," he said, "I want to ask you something and I want a truthful answer or none at all."

The cowgirl blinked, puzzled by the man's sober tone.

"Of course, Roy. What's bothering you?"

Roy found it difficult to harbor any suspicions about this pretty young woman whose efforts had just saved his life, but he was unable to shake off the memory of John Whetlaw's murder at the hands of the Talking Skull. He could not help remembering that the killer who had hidden himself in the Haunted Mission's bell tower had worn a scarlet shirt with crescent pockets, a shirt identical to the one which Texanna was now wearing.

"Texanna, were you anywhere near High Gate yesterday?"

Texanna's candid amber eyes met his without wavering.

"Why, yes. I often ride into the northern hills. The view is so wonderful at the old Spanish padres' mission up on the ridge."

Roy was thoughtful for a moment. He wished more than he could say that Texanna had reassured him that she had been nowhere near the Haunted Mission yesterday.

"When you were there," he said finally, choosing his words with care, "did you see or hear anything unusual around the ruins of the Spanish mission?"

Texanna answered without hesitation, "No. I didn't actually ride up to the Haunted Mission yesterday. I haven't been inside the ruins for several weeks, as a matter of fact."

Suddenly the girl thought of something, for her expression changed. "Oh—I did hear the mission bell give one ring, around noon," she said. "Like an Angelus ringing from a cathedral at midday. That's what the Mexican peons in the Basin think it is when the wind or something rings one of the Haunted Mission bells—they think the ghost of some long-dead padre is pulling on the bell rope, ringing the Angelus."

Rogers did not join in the girl's amusement at the superstition. He was thinking, *that bell wasn't rung by any wind at noon yesterday. John Whetlaw's*

*killer rang it when he climbed the bell-rope to reach
his ambush spot in the tower. It was just the same
as I heard the bell ring when he left the tower.*

He snapped out of his reverie to see Texanna
watching him closely.

"Daddy told me that your Ranger friend was murdered up at the mission yesterday, Roy," she said
gently. "I'm sorry I can't tell you anything you want
to know. If a killer was waiting up in those ruins
yesterday, it's perhaps lucky I didn't ride up there
as I often do."

They were almost within earshot of the blind
foreman now. Roy said quickly, "That red shirt you
wear, Texanna—I'll be frank. John Whetlaw's ambusher was wearing one just like it. I saw him making his getaway."

The fact that Roy Rogers had thus taken her into
his confidence told Texanna that he had absolved
her of any suspicion.

"I see," she said, scowling seriously. "Well, as I
told you last night, Roy, every rider who ever entered a Gunsight rodeo from Box C, owns one of
these shirts. We had them made especially to identify
our riders."

Roy said in a low voice, "Say nothing of this to
Jingo, if you please, Texanna."

The blind foreman, hearing their approach,
swung his grulla pony around to join them as they

cantered across the sage-dotted Basin floor toward the ranch.

Reaching Box C, Roy unsaddled Trigger and turned the palomino into the cavvy corral. Then, exhausted as he was, he went out to the crew's bath-house to clean up, and from there to the bunkhouse.

Physical weariness made him sleep soundly, and it was the clang of Fung Ling's supper triangle at dusk that roused him. During the afternoon a Mexican servant had laundered his shirt and Levis, but he got fresh clothing and an extra pair of high-heeled boots from his war sack and dressed.

At supper Roy found himself seated next to Jingo Bates. He asked the blind man, "I don't see the wrangler around—Bronco Alamar. Has he been gone all day?"

Jingo shrugged. "Why ask me, Roy? I can't see who's here and who ain't."

Bronco Alamar did not show up at the bunkhouse until long after dark. In answer to a question put to him by one of the cowboys, he said moodily, "Where have I been? None of your business, waddy."

Roy Rogers, stretched out on his bunk to ease the pain of his aching muscles, saw Alamar flash him a look of pure hatred.

Dozing off to sleep, Roy wondered: *Bronc Alamar wasn't around all day. Could he have dressed up in a skeleton suit and challenged me down on the Rio this morning, as the Ghost?*

Thinking further, *Had Bronc Alamar been responsible for putting dummy bullets in his guns while he slept last night?* That thought Roy Rogers carried with him into his sleep, and his rest was disturbed by nightmares of Bronc Alamar wearing the skull mask of the Ghost of Mystery Rancho.

Next morning, immediately after breakfast, Roy Rogers saddled up and headed for Gunsight. He found the town a lawless mining camp and cow town in a Navajada canyon, east of the Box C and built on a considerable elevation from the Basin floor.

Going to the Overland Telegraph office, Rogers sent a message to Ranger headquarters in Austin, letting John Whetlaw's chief know of the Ranger captain's murder.

Then he went over to the morgue where his friend's dead body had been taken yesterday. Turning over sufficient money to take care of John Whetlaw's burial expenses, Roy returned to the hitchrack where he had left Trigger, and rode out of town.

Passing the county jail, he was sorely tempted to go in and introduce himself to Sheriff Tommy Stockton, the lawman who was in love with Texanna Conroy. But it was past noon, and Roy Rogers had urgent business to attend to on the bank of the Rio Grande—business of too dangerous a nature to involve Gunsight's young sheriff.

It was nearing sundown when Roy Rogers reached the granite butte that overlooked the quicksand *sumidero*.

Already the deadly bog of black mire had smoothed over, as smooth as the surrounding earth, the loose, gray sand giving no hint of the deadly peril beneath its surface.

Roy dismounted and led Trigger down into the narrow gulch where the Ghost of Mystery Rancho had vanished yesterday.

Down below the draw's rimrocks, Roy unsaddled Trigger.

Taking leave of his faithful mount, Roy scrambled back up the sloping end of the arroyo, carrying a coil of rawhide rope on his arm, a lariat he had borrowed from the Box C barn that morning.

This time Roy had no intentions of repeating his stunt of yesterday. Instead, he skirted the *sumidero* and climbed up the talus shoulder of the butte until he reached the base of the sheer granite wall.

There was a sharp tooth of rock jutting from the rimrock a dozen feet overhead, and over this rock Roy looped his lasso. Drawing it tight, he got a good grip on the plaited rawhide and, bracing his feet on the eroded surface of the butte, began climbing the rope.

At the rimrock he crawled out on a level ledge

and pulled the forty-foot riata up, coiling it carefully.

From the top of this butte he had a clear view of the Rio Grande and the frowning Chihuahua hills across the river. The Mexican badlands looked forbidding and ominous in the red glare of the sunset.

Over there was the domain of the notorious Mexican smuggler king, Señor Rattlesnake. Unless Roy was mistaken, it was also the hiding place of the Ghost of Mystery Rancho. Perhaps the Ghost would turn out to be Señor Rattlesnake, but Roy doubted that. He believed that in his two days at Mystery Rancho he had made substantial progress toward solving the riddle. He wondered if the four lawmen who had vanished without trace before Ranger Captain John Whetlaw came had ever visited this butte.

Making his way along the rim of the butte, Roy halted when he was directly over the smoke tree snag and the brush clumps at the inner edge of the quicksand *sumidero*.

He found a heavy boulder and put the loop of his lariat around it, tossing the remainder of the rope over the cliff's brink. There was more than enough rope, he knew, to reach the foot of the smoke tree snag where someone—Señor Rattlesnake, according to Texanna's story—had cut his rope yesterday with the long-bladed knife.

Quivering with excitement, Roy Rogers sat down

on the edge of the cliff, got a good grip on the rope, and slid out into space.

He went hand-over-hand down the rope, his legs unable to touch the weather-polished wall of granite because of an overhanging brow of rock above him.

A moment later his boots struck the top of the brush; then darkness closed in as he slid below the level of the thicket tops, and his cowboots landed on solid rubble.

As his eyes became accustomed to the half-light, Roy located what he had come here to find: the secret door through which Señor Rattlesnake had escaped yesterday.

It was a massive door of hewn logs. He saw rusty, handwrought iron hinges, and remembered how he had heard them creak as the door opened and closed.

In front of this door was an open area, very narrow but high enough to accommodate a man on a horse. This extended out to the quicksand bog's smooth surface.

A huge bronze knob was bolted to the door. Loosening his six-guns in leather, Roy Rogers twisted the knob, fully expecting to find it locked on the inside.

The door swung open with surprising ease, and Roy found himself peering into the gloomy depths of a cavern which sloped off into total darkness.

The fading sunset glow penetrated a few yards

into this tunnel, and Roy saw that it sloped downward at an angle, resembling a mine's drift.

At first glimpse, Roy believed the floor had been covered with planks, which bore the scuff marks of iron horseshoes.

Then, on closer inspection, he discovered that the planks were mounted on iron rollers, these wheels resting in turn on a narrow iron track, similar to the kind miners used for rolling their ore carts out of mine shafts.

The wooden platform, three feet wide, was about twenty feet in length. Studying it, Roy Rogers knew he had solved the riddle of how the Ghost of Mystery Rancho had crossed the quicksand bog.

This wooden gangplank could be trundled out of the cave on its steel track, so that it extended across the *sumidero.* Some accomplice of the Ghost's—Señor Rattlesnake, perhaps—had rolled the gangplank out of the cave yesterday, the Ghost had spurred his horse across it, and then the gangplank had been trundled back behind this secret door. Because of the brush growing outside, no eye could spot the door in the cliff from the far rim of the quicksand.

Where did the tunnel lead? There was only one way to find out. Stepping into the fusty tunnel, Roy Rogers closed the big door behind him and then groped his way into the cave's sooty blackness.

CHAPTER VIII

SOUTH OF THE RIO GRANDE

Not daring to light a match, Roy groped his way along the wooden gangplank until he reached its end. Feeling around in the total darkness, he discovered that the steel tracks ended here.

Drawing a gun in readiness to meet any danger this cavern might hold, Roy slid the finger tips of his left hand along the rocky wall of the tunnel and headed down its dank, echoing length.

Counting his paces, Roy estimated that he had gone a hundred yards before the roof-steep slope of the tunnel leveled off.

Water seeping from the rock ceiling of the cavern gave Roy an idea. This cavern had been chiseled out of bedrock, *under the Rio Grande river!* Perhaps at this very moment he had passed from Texas into Mexico!

The ceiling of the tunnel was higher than Roy could reach, so he knew it would accommodate a mounted rider. It was nowhere narrower than six feet and the floor paved with crushed rock.

Some fifty paces farther on, Roy felt the tunnel

begin to lift on an upward grade, similar to the one on the Texas side of the river.

From the sodden echoes which hit his ears, Roy knew he was approaching a dead end of some kind. He put his hands in front of him, moving with extreme stealth, being careful of his footing on the wet gravel.

Then, at the top of the slope, he butted into a wall of heavy logs. Fumbling about, he traced the outlines of a door similar to the one on the Texas end of the cavern.

Through cracks in the logs he could glimpse the cold remote glitter of stars in the Mexican sky, feel the icy breath of the breeze sweeping along the Rio's gorge.

Heart pumping with excitement, Roy Rogers groped for and found a metal knob. He turned it, again fearful of finding any further passage blocked by a heavy lock. But again the door responded to his push, and he stepped out into the Mexican starlight.

The door to the cavern under the Rio Grande swung shut gently of its own weight. Like its counterpart on the north end of the tunnel, this secret door was masked behind heavy brush.

A path led through this chaparral, and Roy saw its course twisting up a rocky slope to vanish around a bend into a canyon.

Climbing the slope, every sense tuned to a high

pitch, Roy paused to glance behind him.

There was the Rio Grande, reflecting the myriad stars of the Milky Way and the Big Dipper. Across the river he could see the butte where the quick-sand bog was located. And there dimly he could see the line of Box C's drift fence where he and Texanna had seen the Ghost of Mystery Rancho riding his black horse up this very path where he now stood.

Aware of the certain death which awaited him if he was discovered south of the United States border, Roy Rogers reached up to unpin John Whetlaw's Ranger badge, and pocketed it. The moonlight flash-ing on that silver star might betray him to the eyes of smuggler sentinels posted along this trail.

Ready for anything, Roy continued on up the curving ribbon of ash-gray trail into the canyon. Here, beyond sight of the Rio Grande, a sense of lostness and complete loneliness assailed the cowboy.

The canyon narrowed until he could see but a narrow, ragged strip of sky, dusted with its diamond-point stars. A breeze sucked down this canyon, car-rying to his nostrils the scent of wood smoke.

Down in the canyon's pit, a stream brawled over its rocky rapids, sluicing its way into the Rio Grande. This trail was little more than a ledge following a fault-seam in the cliff. A single misstep would dash him to his doom on the jagged granite fangs lost in the darkness below.

Hugging the canyon wall, Roy continued along the trail, the odor of burning wood stronger in his nostrils by the minute.

Then, rounding a hairpin turn of the canyon, Roy saw yellow lighted windows blooming against the ebony blackness of the gorge wall some fifty yards ahead.

He heard horses munching hay in some near-by barn; where the canyon widened he saw the pole rails of a corral, resembling bleached bones in what starshine penetrated this deep cleft in the mountains.

This must be Señor Rattlesnake's smuggler den, the thought speared through Roy's brain. *I'll bet I'm the first gringo who ever laid eyes on this spot!*

With complete caution, Roy worked his way along the corral fence, careful to keep out of the fan-shaped spread of lamplight coming from the building ahead.

A mutter of human voices reached his ears above the organ roar of the creek in the canyon below this outlaw lair. Roy inched his way toward the lighted windows until he made out the dim outlines of an adobe and stone *jacal* hut, of the type Mexican peons throughout Chihuahua province lived in.

The wood smoke he had smelled farther down the canyon came from the squat stone chimney of this shack. At closer range, other odors began to blend with that smoke: rancid bacon and chili and onions.

Pausing every few feet to wait and watch, Roy

finally gained the corner of the cabin. It was about fifteen feet square, with the doorway opening onto the path he had left back at the corral.

Built against the cliff wall was a lean-to barn roofed over with maguay leaves; inside that barn the smuggler band apparently kept their horses.

With infinite caution, testing each step against the possibility of kicking some object or breaking a twig that would betray his presence here to hostile ears, Roy inched his way along the side of the hut, approaching a narrow loophole which served as a ventilating window.

Reaching it, Roy took off his wide-brimmed Stetson and cautiously peered around the edge of the thick adobe wall.

What he saw inside the lamplit shack made the hairs crawl on the nape of his neck.

A group of men were eating tortillas and drinking pulque at a long wooden table. The rafters were hung with gourds and drying peppers and slabs of bacon; an oil lamp with a green shade threw its cone of yellow light on the men, and the dingy interior of the room pulsed to the flickering glow of a fire on a low hearth, piled high with mesquite chunks.

Most of the diners—numbering ten in all—were Mexicans who still wore their bright serapes and steeple-crowned sombreros while they wolfed their food. But at least three of the men were Chinese

Roy Inched Toward the Window

with skull caps and black gowns and lon...
queues.

Dominating the men at the head of the...
facing the loophole outside of which R...
crouched, was a strikingly costumed Mex...
a ropey mustache and pockmarked face.

This Mexican wore a green velvet jac...
shirt richly adorned with gold braid. Roy...
the flash of rubies which encrusted the bu...
two revolvers holstered at his thighs.

The Mexican's sleeves were rolled ba...
elbows, and Roy Rogers saw that his righ...
tattooed from elbow to wrist with the lik...
coiled rattlesnake.

This, then, was Señor Rattlesnake—k...
border outlawry, the most-wanted sm...
Mexico! These other Chinese and Mexi...
his gang, no doubt. This man in his gaud...
was the outlaw who had slashed Roy Ro...
yesterday, dropping him into the *sumide*...

At that moment there was a lull in the...
tion, and another figure moved into the...
Roy's vision.

The Ghost of Mystery Rancho!

Roy stifled a gasp as he stared at the s...
which this man wore, the black-and-white...
his skeleton costume. The Ghost, he noted...
was the same general height and build of...

cavvy wrangler, Bronc Alamar. Did that skull mask
conceal the surly rider's leering face?

As the Ghost rounded the table and put his back
to the warmth of the fireplace, still another man
walked into the range of Roy Rogers's view from the
loophole.

This last was a Chinese. His identity came as an
astounding surprise to Roy Rogers, for he was none
other than Buck Conroy's ranch cook, Fung Ling!

Fung Ling's bland Oriental face gave no sign as to
whether he was a prisoner of the Ghost's in this
smuggler den south of the border. His long-nailed
hands were thrust into the loose, baggy sleeves of his
black gown, and his eyes were like black bits of flint.

"All right, Fung Ling," the Ghost of Mystery
Rancho broke the quiet. "What do the gentlemen
from Cathay want to tell us?"

The Ghost spoke in Spanish, but when Fung Ling
addressed the three Chinamen who were eating rice
from bowls with their ivory chopsticks, he spoke in
singsong Cantonese dialect.

Señor Rattlesnake stopped eating, giving the Chinese cook his full attention. The Ghost stood in the
background, waiting for Fung Ling to interpret
what the Chinese men were saying.

When they had finished, Fung Ling turned to the
Ghost and relayed his information in a nasal-ac-
cented Mexican jargon.

"The honorable Chee Fu he say rice paper come in small bundles, señor," Fung Ling said. "They sell paper they brought by clipper ship from China to Señor Rattlesnake in return for bars of Mexican silver."

Roy Rogers saw the Ghost turn to Señor Rattlesnake. The Mexican smuggler said gruffly, "Fung Ling, tell our friends from across the sea that the silver bars are ready for them."

Fung Ling passed this information along to the Orientals who stood and bowed formally.

"*Bueno*," the Ghost said. "Now we will handle it this way. Pedro, Pablo, Heraclio, Gonzales and Flores are miners who work at the diggings over in the Navajadas above Gunsight. They will carry the bundles of rice paper over to the Texas side of the Rio. They will follow the rim of the Basin to the road to town. At Gunsight, Pedro will turn the rice paper over to our friend Furtado Gomez at the Tres Coronas saloon. It's as simple as that."

Señor Rattlesnake chuckled low in his throat.

"And Furtado Gomez will convert this illegal shipment of rice paper into gringo money," the smuggler boasted. "I am paying these Chinese smugglers a hundred thousand dollars in silver for this counterfeit paper. But Furtado will print nearly a million dollars' worth of fake five-dollar United States bills. A neat profit, eh, Señor Ghost?"

Roy Rogers saw the Ghost of Mystery Rancho's eyes flash behind the skull mask.

"*Si*, Señor Rattlesnake. And the stupid gringo border guards will not think to search any of these Mexican miners on their way to Gunsight—miners who have their passports in order, miners who have been searched without success so many times before."

Roy Rogers ducked back out of sight as he saw the Mexicans come to their feet.

"We'll leave here in half an hour," he heard the Ghost instructing the Gunsight miners. "One package of rice paper for each of you—easily carried, but more precious than diamonds."

Above the babble of sound inside, where the Oriental smugglers were turning over their counterfeit-money paper in return for Señor Rattlesnake's silver, Roy Rogers's brain was spinning with plans.

Here on the Mexican side of the Rio Grande, he had no legal right to arrest these smugglers, even though he had caught the gang red-handed in the act of trading for contraband.

In another thirty minutes, the Ghost of Mystery Rancho would lead his five miners from Gunsight through the tunnel under the Rio Grande.

And although he did not know how he was going to manage it, Roy intended to arrest the Ghost and his accomplices before the hour was out!

CHAPTER IX

ROY'S DISGUISE

Inside Señor Rattlesnake's hut, the three black-queued Chinese who had come to a Mexican seaport by clipper ship from the Orient were busy carrying out their part in the smuggling pact. Rogers saw each of the men produce small bundles wrapped in tissue paper from their black gowns.

Those packages, Roy knew, contained Chinese rice paper which came closer to the silk-threaded paper used by the United States government in its printing of greenbacks than any paper produced by American counterfeiters.

He recalled what John Whetlaw had told him on their ride west from San Antonio—how the United States was being flooded with bogus currency believed smuggled into Texas across the Rio Grande. In some way, Whetlaw believed, this contraband traffic was connected with the Ghost and Mystery Rancho. Five lawmen, including Whetlaw, had died before cracking that secret which was being unfolded before Roy's eyes tonight.

Señor Rattlesnake placed a couple of pack mule

sacks, fitted with heavy bullhide pouches, on the table. From them, the Mexican outlaw lifted heavy ingots of Sonora silver which he turned over to the waiting Oriental smugglers.

Meanwhile, the Ghost of Mystery Rancho was passing out bundles of counterfeit rice paper to the five Mexicans who would transport it to Gunsight.

While Señor Rattlesnake and the Chinese were finishing their transaction, the Ghost summoned his Mexican miners and led them out into the night.

Roy Rogers crouched invisible in the darkness behind the hut, watching the Ghost and his henchmen head for the horse barn. When they had gone inside, Roy Rogers slipped out of his hiding place and, hugging the base of the cliff, made his way to the corrals. He was once more wearing his Ranger star.

A lantern gave a feeble light inside the barn. Concealing himself behind a haystack, Roy peered through a barn window and saw the Ghost busy saddling a black horse—the one he had been riding yesterday when he challenged Roy and Texanna Conroy.

As the black wheeled around, Roy caught sight of the brand it wore on its glossy coat. A *Box C!* Buck Conroy, then, owned the horse that the Ghost of Mystery Rancho was using. In a few hours, that stallion would be mingling with Bronc Alamar's cavvy over at Conroy's corral.

One by one the Mexican miners from Gunsight saddled their horses and led them out into the moonlight to where the Ghost was waiting in front of Señor Rattlesnake's hut. There was only one Mexican left in the barn now, and he was having trouble getting his saddle cinch adjusted to suit him.

The germ of a bold idea came to Roy Rogers, as he watched the Mexican inside the barn.

Coming away from the haystack, Roy Rogers climbed a compost pile heaped under the stable window.

A six-gun drawn, Roy Rogers slipped through the window and landed on the straw-scattered floor of the barn with the lithe ease of a cat.

The Mexican was standing behind his horse, a strawberry roan, busy tightening the latigo, one stirrup hooked over the dish-shaped Texas horn.

Roy Rogers moved swiftly past the row of stalls where Señor Rattlesnake's horses were feeding, sur- prising the Mexican miner in the act of reaching for his reins to lead the roan outdoors to join the others.

Whirling, the Mexican's eyes went round with terror as he spotted the shining badge of a Texas Ranger on the shirt of this stranger.

Even as the Mexican opened his mouth to shout a warning, Roy's gun lifted and fell, striking the miner's skull with a sodden, meaty impact.

Knocked cold, the Mexican slumped on the stable floor.

Holstering his gun, Roy worked swiftly. He pulled the steeple-crowned, ball-tassled sombrero from the unconscious man's head and put it on his own, scaling his gray Stetson into a vacant manger.

Then he removed the miner's serape and the poncho which the man wore against the chill of the night. When he had donned the Mexican's garments, Roy's own clothing was concealed.

At that instant, the Ghost's harsh voice rang out sharply from in front of the stable.

"*Andale,* Pedro! Hurry up! What's keeping you?"

Pitching his voice low in the gutteral jargon of a *pelado,* Roy called back, "I come, Señor—I come pronto," and led the roan out of the lantern-lighted stable.

The disguised American cowboy was a black shape against the barn doorway as he swung into stirrups and spurred the strawberry out to join the group gathered around the Ghost.

Señor Rattlesnake strode out of his hut and reached up to shake the Ghost's hand.

"Give Furtado Gomez my best wishes," chuckled the Mexican *contrabandista.* "Next time you cross the Rio, send Gomez with you, *amigo.*"

The Ghost waved in farewell and spurred his black Box C-branded stallion off down the ledge trail, motioning for the Gunsight miners to follow. Roy Rogers brought up the rear, his disguise undetected.

Not until they were halfway down the canyon did Roy Rogers realize that in his haste to put on Pedro's clothing, he had neglected to pick up Pedro's bundle of rice paper, which the unlucky Mexican had no doubt stowed in a pocket of his bell-bottomed velvet *pantalones*.

But that did not matter. If all went well tonight, Roy knew he would arrive in Gunsight for a meeting with Gomez who was a counterfeiter on the side, with plenty of smuggling evidence to turn over to Sheriff Tommy Stockton. One more parcel of the Chinese paper would not matter.

Coming out of the canyon mouth within sight of the Rio Grande, the Ghost headed directly into the chaparral which concealed the mouth of the underground passage which led to the Texas bank.

Leaning from stirrups, the skeleton-suited Ghost pulled the heavy slab door open and backed his horse away while the five Mexicans, Roy Rogers in their midst, spurred their mounts into the inky-black throat of the tunnel.

As soon as Roy's strawberry roan was inside the cavern, the Ghost spurred after them, closing Señor Rattlesnake's secret door behind them.

Inside this tunnel the beat of iron-shod hoofs on

rubble set up a clamoring set of echoes, nearly deafening them. Reaching up, Roy Rogers discovered that he could barely touch the jagged rock ceiling of the passage.

Strung out in single file, their ponies' hoofs shedding sparks from the rocky floor, the cavalcade reached the foot of the decline and leveled off.

Water dripping on his sombrero brim gave Roy Rogers an uncanny feeling of danger. It was a weird and unreal feeling to know he was literally riding a horse under the great river which formed the boundary between Mexico and Texas.

A charge of dynamite at this point would bring the river flooding into this tunnel, Roy thought. *Sooner or later that is exactly what the United States Border Patrol will do to shut off this smuggling leak into America.*

With the Ghost of Mystery Rancho bringing up the rear, the file of riders slowed down as their mounts started up the steep angle of the north slope.

When the lead rider reached the end of the gangplank on iron rails he reined up and the others followed suit.

The Ghost barked an order in Spanish and spurred past the group, his stirrup leathers brushing the poncho which Roy Rogers was wearing.

Reaching the end of the black tunnel, the Ghost moved a hidden lever and the north door of the cavern swung open, giving Roy a view of the silhouetted Mexicans against the moonlit background of the quicksand bog.

Chains clanked noisily in the darkness, and Roy knew that some system of block and tackle and gears was trundling the wooden plank walk out of the tunnel to form a bridge across the dangerous surface of the *sumidero* outside.

" 'Sta bueno," came the Ghost's low voice as he spurred out onto the spur-splintered gangway. "Follow, and keep quiet."

One by one the Mexican miners put their horses on the wooden walkway.

Unpleasant memories of his own ordeal in the quicksand yesterday flooded through Roy Rogers as his strawberry roan picked its way carefully along the narrow plank walk over the *sumidero's* lurking black sands.

A moment later his horse was leaping off the gangplank onto solid earth at the north edge of the bog.

Roy Rogers, thankful for the blot of shadow which his wide-brimmed sombrero cast over his face in the moonlight, reined up with the other Mexicans.

"All right," the Ghost said. "You know what to do. Ride directly to the *Tres Coronas cantina* in Gunsight and turn over the bundles of rice paper to Señor Gomez. He will pay you for your night's work."

The Mexicans grunted their understanding, Roy

joining in the chorus. Without delay, the miners headed toward Tomahawk Basin, leaving the Ghost of Mystery Rancho behind.

For a moment, indecision struck Roy Rogers. He had hoped against hope that the man he most wanted to arrest, the Ghost, would accompany these smugglers to town. Instead, the skull-masked outlaw was even now heading back across the quicksand bog's gangplank, no doubt to trundle the wooden structure back out of sight and close the tunnel door.

It was in Roy's power to put his guns on the Ghost now. The other Mexicans, so far as he knew, did not carry weapons.

On the other hand, it was important to follow this thing through to the end and be able to assist Sheriff Stockton of Gunsight in capturing these smugglers and the boss counterfeiter, Furtado Gomez.

Now that he knew the secret of the Ghost's hideout in Mexico, Roy knew he could storm Señor Rattlesnake's den with a posse at any time he chose.

Having made up his mind, Rogers spurred Pedro's roan into a jog trot and set off after the other Mexicans. The next time he twisted in saddle for a look at the quicksand *sumidero,* it was to see that the Ghost of Mystery Rancho had already rolled the gangplank back into the secret cavern.

CHAPTER X

The Ghost of Mystery Rancho traveled back through the tunnel under the Rio Grande—a tunnel partly man-made by the Spanish conquerers hundreds of years ago, partly the dried-up passage of an underground river—and headed back to Señor Rattlesnake's canyon lair.

He found the Chinese smugglers already in saddle, with pack horses laden with Señor Rattlesnake's silver ingots.

Bidding his countrymen farewell was the Box C cook, Fung Ling. Fung Ling rarely displayed his emotions. But now his eyes were moist with tears as he shook hands with the Cantonese smugglers and spoke to them in his native tongue.

The Ghost and Señor Rattlesnake heard but one word they could recognize in this singsong recital. Mazatlan. That was the port on the west seacoast of Mexico where the smugglers would board a Hong Kong junk for the return voyage across the Pacific.

It was obvious that Fung Ling would have traded ten years of his life to have accompanied these Chinese back to his native province. Fung Ling had come to America as a young man to work on a transcontinental railroad; he had wound up as a cook on Buck Conroy's ranch.

As long as he was under the grip of the Ghost of Mystery Rancho, Fung Ling knew he had little hope of returning to the land of his ancestors across the sea.

The Ghost was grinning evilly behind his skull mask as he saw the Chinese smugglers depart, leaving Fung Ling behind.

"All right, Fung Ling," the Ghost said gruffly. "We've got to get back to the Box C. It isn't good for either of us to be absent too long on mysterious business. Sometimes I think Texanna wonders why you make so many trips to Gunsight, especially when the sheriff doesn't see you in town at any of the Chinese hangouts."

Fung Ling's sandaled feet shuffled off_toward the barn to get his horse for the return ride across Tomahawk Basin.

The Ghost and Señor Rattlesnake were conversing in low tones out in front of the adobe cabin when they heard a high-pitched squeal of terror issue from the horse barn.

Something had scared the Chinese cook, for he came racing out of the lantern-lighted barn with his queue flying behind him.

"Señor Pedro lies dead in the barn, Señor!" yelled

the Box C cook, skidding to a halt in front of the two outlaw chiefs. "By the bones of my ancestors, that is so!"

Under his skull mask, the Ghost's face tightened.

"That is impossible," rasped the outlaw. "I counted the miners as they left the tunnel door. There were five of them. Pedro cannot be left behind."

Fung Ling waggled his head frantically, pointing toward the barn. "Pedro lies dead on the barn floor—it is true!"

The Ghost leaped from horseback to join Señor Rattlesnake, who was racing toward the barn.

They reached the doorway together. There, sprawled out on the straw-littered floor of the barn, lay the motionless figure of Pedro—minus his sombrero, poncho, and serape. Jutting from a hip pocket of his velvet pants was the bundle of Chinese rice paper Pedro was supposed to deliver to the counterfeiter in Gunsight.

Señor Rattlesnake was the first to reach Pedro's side. Rolling him over, the boss smuggler saw the bleeding gash on the miner's scalp, saw a pulse throbbing in his brown throat.

"The peon is still alive," Señor Rattlesnake snarled. "He has had an accident. Fung Ling, bring an *olla* of water from the house—and a bottle of pulque."

"Whoever did this thing to Pedro must have put

"He Is Alive," Señor Rattlesnake Snarled

on Pedro's clothing as a disguise," the Ghost said hoarsely. "That means an impostor is riding to Gunsight with my *compañeros* tonight—"

Fung Ling returned from Señor Rattlesnake's house with a bottle of pulque in one hand and an *olla* of water in the other.

Señor Rattlesnake seized the *olla* and dumped its contents over Pedro's head.

A moment later the Mexican's black eyes blinked open and he sat up, groaning heavily and rubbing the egg-sized lump on his skull.

The Ghost of Mystery Rancho squatted beside Pedro and forced the mouth of the pulque bottle between his lips. After a couple of gulps of the fiery drink, Pedro rallied enough to talk.

"A gringo hit me with his gon, señores. As I was about to lead my *caballo* out of the barn. That is all I know."

At that moment the Chinese cook stepped out of a horse stall, carrying a gray, cleft-crown Stetson which he had found in a manger.

Without a word, he handed the Stetson to the Ghost, who turned it over for a glance at the leather sweatband inside the hat. Punched through the band was a name: *Roy Rogers*.

"Señor Rogers—the young Texas Ranger who is investigating Mystery Rancho!" gasped the Ghost, handing the Stetson to Señor Rattlesnake. "He either swam the Rio Grande or discovered our tunnel, *amigo*. Roy Rogers must have spied on our meeting tonight!"

Señor Rattlesnake's dusky face had become two shades paler. He whirled with a jingle of sunflower spurs and ran over to where his own mount, a big steel-dust gelding was peacefully munching oats.

"We've got to catch up with those miners before they reach Gunsight!" Señor Rattlesnake yelled, dragging a silver-mounted saddle from a stall hook. "If Roy Rogers is riding in disguise, it may be too late to save our *amigos*."

Five minutes later, the Ghost and Señor Rattlesnake, accompanied by Pedro and Fung Ling, were galloping down the narrow ledge trail toward the Rio Grande with total disregard for the chances of plunging into the canyon.

Going through the Rio Grande tunnel at top speed, they fretted at the necessary delay of getting the gangplank over the *sumidero,* and without bothering to hide this evidence of their secret cavern, they galloped out into Tomahawk Basin.

Thundering hoofs echoed across the moonlit prairie as they headed northeast toward the remote twinkle of lights marking Gunsight. Off to the north were the lights of Buck Conroy's ranch.

Three miles farther on, at the base of the foothill spurs, they caught sight of the five riders heading toward Gunsight. Whipping and spurring their jaded horses for more speed, the four pursuing riders rapidly cut down the Mexicans' lead.

The drumming beat of hoofs reached Roy Rogers's ears and brought a grim feeling of foreboding. Was it possible that Pedro had been discovered so soon?

He thrust a hand under his poncho to grip the stock of a six-gun at his hip.

So far, the four other Mexicans had no idea but what he was their friend, Pedro. But if those following riders meant trouble—

Then the sound of hoofs was swallowed up abruptly, and Roy Rogers relaxed. The riders had not been trailing him from Señor Rattlesnake's lair, apparently; they had turned off the trail in the direction of Buck Conroy's ranch.

The Mexicans appeared to be in no hurry to get to Gunsight. They were foxtrotting their horses along, keeping their silence—a thing for which Pedro's double was thankful, for Roy Rogers knew that while he could speak fluent Spanish, his voice would not match Pedro's.

The five riders were topping a cactus-dotted ridge against which a tall cottonwood spread its gnarled branches against the sky, when four riders spurred suddenly from an arroyo and rode out to block the Gunsight trail.

Roy Rogers sucked in a gasp of despair as he rec- ognized Señor Rattlesnake, the Ghost, Fung Ling, and Pedro, the Mexican whose clothes he was wear- ing.

Too late, this cowboy who wore a Texas Ranger star under his serape realized that the Ghost had taken a short-cut to head them off.

Snarling an order for the other Mexicans to rein aside, the Ghost headed straight toward Roy Rogers, moonlight glinting off his leveled six-guns.

"That ees heem!" shouted Pedro, pointing toward the rider who wore his battered sombrero. "That ees Roy Rogers!"

Hemmed in by leveled guns, Roy Rogers had no choice but to lift his arms in surrender or be shot from saddle instantly.

Señor Rattlesnake spurred in swiftly from the right and with the barrel of a rifle, knocked off Roy's sombrero to expose the cowboy's handsome gringo face, plainly visible in the moon rays.

At the same moment Pedro came alongside his other stirrup and reached out savagely to retrieve his serape and poncho.

The other Mexicans stared goggle-eyed at the Texas Ranger badge on the shirt of the rider who had accompanied them more than halfway to their destination, a rider they had assumed was their friend Pedro.

"All right, Ranger Rogers!" snarled the Ghost of Mystery Rancho in his thick gutteral voice. He spoke in English this time, with a heavy Mexican accent which might have been, or might not have been, that of the Box C cavvy wrangler, Bronc Alamar. "Anything to say about this hoax, Rogers?"

Señor Rattlesnake's rifle barrel hooked under the curved butt of first one, then the other of Roy's .45's, flipping them out of holsters to hit the dirt.

"Not much I can say, Ghost." The cowboy grinned bleakly. "I gambled and lost."

Without warning, Señor Rattlesnake struck Roy behind the ear with his Winchester barrel.

Stunned, Roy felt himself dive from stirrups and hit the ground with a hard impact.

He was vaguely aware of Pedro lashing his arms behind his back with a sisal riata, then hauling him to his feet. Wobbly-legged because of the blow on his skull, Roy stared around to find himself completely surrounded by enemies. Fung Ling had picked up his Colt six-guns and had thrust them in the big pockets of his Chinese robe.

"We're very lucky, *amigos,*" the Ghost was saying. "If we hadn't discovered Pedro in time, this Texas Ranger would have taken all of you to jail—and Furtado Gomez's counterfeit shop would have been discovered by the law."

Señor Rattlesnake's white teeth flashed in the

moonlight as he stared at Roy Rogers. A trickle of blood seeped from the cut the Mexican smuggler's gun barrel had put under Roy's hair.

"Yonder cottonwood makes a handy hangtree," Señor Rattlesnake said. "Or will you shoot this *Rangero,* Señor Ghost, and throw his body in the Well of Bones along with the other gringo lawmen who came to Mystery Rancho?"

Roy felt his heart hammering his ribs with excitement. In spite of the sense of swift doom which froze his blood, Roy was taking a keen interest in what the Mexican smuggler king had just said regarding the fate of the four lawmen who had been killed ahead of John Whetlaw.

"We'll hang him here," the Ghost said, "and leave his body for the buzzards to pick. It will be a warning to other star-toters."

Fung Ling produced a lariat from his saddle, and as Roy watched, the Chinaman's long-nailed fingers deftly fashioned a hangman's knot.

The Chinese cook came very close to Roy Rogers as he fitted the deadly noose over the cowboy's head. He drew the loop tight around Roy's throat and backed off.

The Ghost of Mystery Rancho prodded Roy in the back with his Colt muzzle and Roy found himself stumbling off the trail toward the big cottonwood.

Reaching a spot directly below a heavy horizontal limb which grew some ten feet off the ground, Roy Rogers was halted by his captors.

He watched dully as Fung Ling flipped the hang-rope over that cottonwood limb, tossing the free end of the rope to the Ghost of Mystery Rancho.

Then Fung Ling came back to Roy Rogers and adjusted the five-rope roll of the hangman's knot carefully alongside the doomed man's left temple.

"It is ready, señores!" the Chinaman said grimly. "Death to this Ranger who would have jailed us all!"

Roy Rogers felt the slack of the rope pull up. Señor Rattlesnake and two of the Mexican miners were helping the Ghost at the other end of the rope.

"Any last requests, Roy?" leered the Ghost. "You've got exactly fifteen seconds to live."

Roy Rogers squared his shoulders, flexed his arm muscles under the tight knots which the Chinese ranch cook had tied behind his back.

"Only one thing, Ghost," the cowboy said, his voice holding no suggestion of tremor. "I'd die easier if I had one look at the face behind that skull mask."

The Ghost shook his head. "Not even Señor Rattlesnake knows my secret," he said.

Roy laughed hollowly. "What's the matter, Bronc Alamar—afraid to t—"

The Ghost yelled an order, and the men heaved

hard on the hangrope. Roy's shout was cut off by the strangling rope as he was jerked off the ground, his head inches below the cottonwood limb.

Roy's booted legs did their gruesome dance in mid-air. No further sound came from him. The brutal deed was finished.

Without lowering their victim's body, the Ghost and Señor Rattlesnake tied the hangrope's other end tightly to the trunk of the cottonwood.

"All right," the Ghost of Mystery Rancho addressed the grinning Mexicans. "It was a narrow escape, but the *Rangero* is dead now. Head for town and deliver your packages to Gomez."

Pedro, who had retrieved his own sombrero, hurled the gray Stetson up at Roy Rogers's slowly-revolving body with a defiant laugh. Then he joined the other lynchers as they walked down to the Gunsight trail and mounted.

The Mexicans continued toward Gunsight town, vanishing over the hill. Fung Ling and the Ghost of Mystery Rancho headed in the opposite direction, toward Box C ranch.

Before topping the last ridge overlooking Tomahawk Basin, the Chinese who had been the key figure in this hanging bee turned in saddle for a last look at the cottonwood on the ridge.

Roy Rogers had quit kicking now. His hanging body was limp, swaying in the gentle breeze.

CHAPTER XI

FUNG LING'S RIDE

It was in the gray light of the false dawn that Fung Ling and the Ghost reached the outskirts of Box C. As was usual on the night rides this pair frequently took into Mexico, the skull-masked outlaw reined up and turned to the Chinese cook.

"Get along to the bunkhouse," the masked outlaw said gruffly. "I was beginning to have my doubts about your loyalty, Fung Ling. But the way you helped hang Roy Rogers tonight has restored you to my favor."

Fung Ling's round face was completely without expression.

"Señor Logers was my fliend," he said simply. "I did not wish to see him die by torture. That is why I helped give the *Rangero* a swift and merciful death."

The Chinese cook started his horse forward, then reined up and said to the waiting Ghost, "The hour is such that I will go directly to the cookhouse to start my fires for breakfast, Señor."

The Ghost nodded approval and Fung Ling cantered on into the ranch grounds. He well knew why his master in outlawry made him go on ahead; it

110

gave the Ghost the opportunity to strip off his skull mask and skeleton costume without betraying his identity. For, as the Ghost had told Roy Rogers a moment before the hanging, none of his accomplices knew who he was. His disguise was the Ghost's greatest safety.

Turning into the Box C horse barn, Fung Ling off-saddled. Instead of continuing on to the cookhouse, he waited in the barn's odorous dark until he saw the Ghost turn his black stallion into Bronc Alamar's cavvy corral.

Then, moving like a shadow, the Ghost—no longer wearing his costume and skull mask, but not to be identified at this distance—disappeared around the horse barn. Whether he would go to the main house, or whether he would turn into the bunkhouse, Fung Ling did not know.

After an interval, the Chinese cook saddled a fresh horse and rode away from Box C, headed toward the border. Before the sun spilled its golden flood over the jagged crests of the Navajada range, Fung Ling was out of sight of Conroy's place.

The Chinese cook had a very definite purpose in riding toward the Rio Grande. He was carrying out a whispered request of Roy Rogers—to recover the cowboy's palomino, Trigger, from the gulch beyond the quicksand bog.

No member of the lynching party had known that

Fung Ling and Roy Rogers exchanged whispers. They had accomplished this while the Chinese was fitting the hangnoose about Roy's throat.

Being a Chinese, Fung Ling was loyal to any man who had befriended him in the past. And Roy Rogers had, at great personal risk to himself, rescued Fung Ling from the choking hands of the bullying wrangler, Bronc Alamar, the first night Roy was a member of the Box C crew.

Roy had befriended this Chinese out of the sense of justice which had ruled his own life, and in so doing had made a savage enemy of Bronc Alamar. Fung Ling would never forget that.

Reaching the quicksand *sumidero,* beyond which lay the key to Señor Rattlesnake's hide-out across the Rio Grande, Fung Ling spurred over to the near-by gulch.

Roy Rogers's horse whickered a greeting as Fung Ling dismounted and adjusted the ornate silver-mounted saddle. Then, picking up Trigger's reins, Fung Ling remounted and led the palomino out of the draw.

Knowing Roy's horse was thirsty, Fung Ling headed for the Rio and let the palomino drink. Then, squinting against the intense level glare of the Texas sun poised over the Navajada summit, he headed toward Gunsight town, leading Trigger.

Fung Ling saw no riders on the broad expanse of

Tomahawk Basin as he followed the route taken by Roy Rogers and the four Mexican miners last night. The Box C crew, he knew, would be at breakfast now.

One of their number—perhaps Buck Conroy himself—was the Ghost without his disguise. If that individual discovered that Fung Ling was not in his kitchen, Fung Ling knew what that would mean—death for a traitor.

An hour later Fung Ling caught sight of the cottonwood tree on the ridge which marked the halfway point to town. High in the Texas sky, red-necked *zopilote* buzzards were wheeling in tight spirals over the cottonwood. Those scavengers of the badlands had spotted Roy Rogers swinging under that hangman's tree.

With Trigger trailing, Fung Ling spurred his Box C pony into a gallop. He did not rein in until he had reached the scene of last night's hanging bee.

The full strike of the morning sun was on Roy Rogers's face, but there was a broad grin on the cowboy's mouth, and his blue eyes were alive and vital, warm in their relief at seeing his Chinese friend.

"Reckon I'm the first man in history," chuckled Roy Rogers from his elevated position, "who was ever glad to see his hangman, eh, Fung Ling?"

For the first time in many years—the first time since he had left China as a young man, in fact—the cook's crinkled yellow face broke in an answering smile.

"You my good fliend, Loy Logers," the Chinese cook said, and led Trigger up under the dangling form of the cowboy. "Me never floget favor like you did for Fung Ling in bunkhouse the other night. Me likee you velly much, Loy Logers."

When Trigger was directly beneath Roy's feet, Fung Ling dismounted and walked over to untie the hangman's rope from the limb of the cottonwood.

Then, very gently, he lowered Roy into the saddle.

"You were very ingenious, saving me from a broken neck as you did, Fung Ling," Roy Rogers said. "And to think you played your trick with the hangman's knot under the very eyes of the Ghost and Señor Rattlesnake."

Removing a long-bladed knife from a sleeve of his robe, Fung Ling cut the ropes which bound Roy's arms behind his back.

In broad daylight, the secret of Roy's marvelous survival from lynching was plain to see.

Taking advantage of the moonlight and tricky shadows last night, Fung Ling had cut a three-foot section of rope from his lariat. One end of this rope was tied to Roy Rogers's belt. The other end was knotted securely to the hangrope, inches above the knot.

This extra rope, lying against Roy Rogers's back-bone, had absorbed the shock of his being jerked off the ground, taking Roy's full weight. His heavy leather belt had supported him, instead of his neck.

Now that his hands were free, Roy loosened the hangman's knot from his neck—which Fung Ling had been careful to leave loose enough so that Roy was in no danger of choking—and lifted the noose over his head.

A single stroke of Fung Ling's sharp-edged knife severed the extra rope knotted to his belt.

Massaging his sore wrists and forearms, Roy Rogers reached down gratefully as Fung Ling handed him his twin Colt Peacemaker .45's, which he had picked up at the time of the hanging.

Twirling the cylinders with dextrous thumbs, Roy thrust the six-shooters snugly into holsters.

"Fung Ling, I owe you my life," Roy said, as he saw the cook climb back in saddle. "You ran a risk, bringing Trigger to me. I know that."

The smile faded from Fung Ling's face.

"One good turn deserve another, my fliend," he said. "The other night, I think Blonc Alamar, he plan to stlangle me. You save my life then. I save you last night. Velly good."

Roy Rogers said soberly, "Fung Ling, as a Texas Ranger I should arrest you as a member of Señor Rattlesnake's smuggling gang. But I will not, of

course. I wish you would leave Mystery Rancho, because sooner or later I will have to clean out that
snake den across the Rio. In a showdown, I would
not want to swap lead with you."

Fung Ling's bland face was as blank as a mask.

"You could help me a lot, Fung Ling," Roy Rogers went on, "if you would tell me the identity of the
Ghost of Mystery Rancho."

Fung Ling shook his head.

"I do not know, my fliend Loy," the Chinese said.
"I tell you this: today, I try to leave Mystly Lancho,
leave Amellica. But I beg you, my fliend: do not tly
to fight the Ghost. I do not wish to see you die, my
fliend."

Roy Rogers had many more questions he wanted
to ask this ranch cook who served as Señor Rattlesnake's interpreter south of the border. He wanted
to know about the Well of Bones which the Ghost
had mentioned at the hanging bee last night—the
place where, according to Señor Rattlesnake, the
bodies of the missing American lawmen might be
found.

But Fung Ling, with a wave of farewell, clapped
heels to his horse's flanks and headed down the slope
at a charging gallop.

Roy Rogers was tempted to ride after him, but he
knew that he had a mission to perform in Gunsight
this morning.

"Who Is the Ghost?" Roy Asked Fung Ling

When Fung Ling had vanished over the next ridge, Roy Rogers turned Trigger in the direction of Gunsight. He was glad when he had put the hang-tree behind him.

As Fung Ling headed toward Box C, his heart was filled with an unaccustomed joy. He fully intended to carry out the promise he had made to Roy Rogers: to leave Mystery Rancho forever, and somehow work his way back to China, quitting this life of crime under the Ghost's domination.

It was necessary that he return to Box C. In his war sack he had his life savings, and that money would be necessary to reach San Francisco and book passage on a China-bound schooner. And he also had an urn containing the ashes of a Chinese friend, which he wanted to return to the soil of China to rest with his ancestors.

These thoughts occupied Fung Ling's mind as the Box C cook headed homeward. It came as a rude surprise, then, when a horseman spurred out of a tornillo thicket and blocked his path.

It was the Ghost of Mystery Rancho, once more wearing his skeleton costume and skull mask.

In the Ghost's right hand was a Colt six-gun, its black bore trained on Fung Ling. Around his neck dangled a pair of high-powered field glasses.

"You tricked me last night, Fung Ling!" snarled the Ghost in a blood-curdling voice. "When I found out you didn't cook breakfast, I wondered if you'd come back to cut down Roy Rogers's corpse. Instead, through these binoculars I saw Roy Rogers ride away on Trigger, alive instead of dead."

Fung Ling knew he was doomed. He groped a skinny hand inside his sleeve, feeling for the haft of his knife. There might be a chance that he could hurl that blade into the Ghost's heart before the mystery rider's gun blasted him into eternity. China seemed very far away now.

"Fung Ling," the Ghost went on, speaking as usual in his gutteral Spanish, "you are going to the Well of Bones to join the skeletons of the gringo lawmen who tried to find out who I am. For the first time, I am going to let another look behind my mask. Look at my face, Fung Ling."

So saying, the Ghost of Mystery Rancho tipped up his skull mask to reveal his features.

"You!" gasped Fung Ling, staring incredulously. "*You* cannot be the Ghost of Mystly Lancho—"

Flame spat from the bore of the Ghost's gun, and Fung Ling pitched limply from saddle, a bullet between the eyes. His face still wore the expression of shocked disbelief which had been his when he learned, too late, the secret of the Ghost's identity.

CHAPTER XII

Riding into Gunsight town, Roy Rogers stabled Trigger and headed directly to a restaurant, where a cup of coffee and a plate of ham and eggs relieved his hunger.

Then, having finished his hearty breakfast, the handsome young cowboy made his way to the county jail.

Knocking on the door of the front office, Roy was greeted by a tall young man in a ten-gallon hat, red riding shirt, and batwing chaps. On his breast pocket was pinned a ball-pointed sheriff's star.

"Sheriff Tommy Stockton?" Roy inquired courteously.

The sheriff's blue eyes glinted humorously as he nodded.

"The same. What can I do for you, stranger?"

Roy accepted Stockton's invitation to step into the jail office. Turning to the lawman, he extended his hand and said, "I'm Roy Rogers, Sheriff. Allow me to congratulate you. Miss Texanna tells me you two intend to be married."

Stockton's boyish grin faded over their handshake.

"I—I'm sort of stalling off the wedding," he said,

"until the Ghost of Mystery Rancho has been laid low. I wouldn't want Texanna to be a widow before her wedding bouquet withers. And as long as the Ghost is operating in my county, I'm a marked man for ambush."

"Sheriff," Roy Rogers said, "if you've got the time I have quite a story to tell you."

Stockton waved Roy into a barrel chair, seating himself in a swivel seat beside his battered rolltop desk. The walls of this jail office were papered with reward posters, prominent among which was a red-printed blazer signed by Stockton himself, offering a five-thousand-dollar reward for the capture, dead or alive, of the mysterious outlaw known as the Ghost of Mystery Rancho.

"Texanna told me about your coming to Box C the other day," Stockton said gravely. "Your friend John Whetlaw was buried yesterday. I imagine you had other things to keep you busy or you would have attended the Ranger captain's funeral."

Roy nodded, feeling a pang of grief shoot through him as he realized that he had missed his chance of paying his last respects to the friend he had seen die at Haunted Mission, the man whose Ranger badge was even now pinned to his shirt.

"I *was* slightly busy," Roy said dryly. "I had best begin at the beginning—"

Tersely, Roy described his arrival at High Gate

with Whetlaw and the finding of the message under the Painted Rock. The message, Rogers now believed, had been faked and Buck Conroy's name forged on it. He recounted briefly the circumstances of John Whetlaw's murder by the Talking Skull, holding back only the fact that Whetlaw's killer wore a scarlet shirt identical to that worn by Stockton's fiancée, Texanna Conroy.

He went on to voice his complete trust in Buck Conroy, who had sworn that he had not received Whetlaw's message telling him when he would arrive at High Gate.

"Anyone could have intercepted that telegram—anyone on Box C," Stockton cut in, tugging his lower lip thoughtfully. "We'll have to ask the Overland Telegraph operator who received Whetlaw's wire from San Antone. Maybe he remembers who picked it up and took it out to the ranch—but he's probably forgotten by now."

Roy Rogers went on to describe his first meeting with the Ghost, and his ordeal in the quicksand bog. Stockton's nods at this point in Roy's narrative told the cowboy that either Texanna or Jingo Bates, the blind foreman, had already told the young sheriff about their rescue of Roy from the *sumidero*.

Stockton's face took on a keener interest when he heard of Roy's discovery of the tunnel under the Rio Grande, and of the smugglers' meeting Roy had witnessed last night at Señor Rattlesnake's lair.

Because he wanted to keep inviolate the secret of Fung Ling's artful hangrope trick, Roy passed over that episode entirely, telling Stockton that unforeseen circumstances had prevented him from accompanying the Mexican smugglers on to Gunsight this morning.

"And that's how my investigations stack up so far, Sheriff," Roy concluded his lengthy recital. "I've let the Ghost slip through my fingers, but at least I can tell you that the counterfeiter the government has been searching for so long is right here in town."

Stockton got up and began pacing the floor of the jail office like an animal in a cage.

"Furtado Gomez," the sheriff muttered. "A bad actor, but I've never been able to pin anything on him. His Tres Coronas is the hangout of the Mexicans who work in the mines hereabouts."

Tommy Stockton ceased his nervous pacing and wheeled to face Roy Rogers.

"Could you identify those five Mexicans who smuggled the rice paper into town last night if you saw them again?" Stockton asked anxiously.

Roy nodded. "Sure," he said. "Sure, I could identify them. But don't forget, Tommy—my word against theirs wouldn't hold in court. Unless we can find the evidence on them, we can't convict them of smuggling."

Stockton hitched his gun belts, tonguing his cheek thoughtfully.

"This is Sunday," he said. "The mines aren't working. The Tres Coronas will be full of Mexicans eating and drinking. I have no doubt but what Señor Rattlesnake's smugglers will be among them."

Roy stood up, his own mind having been busy with plans since his arrival in Gunsight.

"At any rate," he said, "I think a search of Furtado Gomez's premises would reveal his counterfeiting plant. How many deputies do you have on duty?"

Stockton scowled. "Only two. Then there is the town marshal, and the Border Patrol has a couple of inspectors on duty here, Gunsight being an official port of entry."

Roy grinned. "Good. That makes seven officers, counting you and me. What are we waiting for?"

The sheriff's brows arched in a startled expression.

"You're suggesting a raid on Gomez's place—without official search warrants? Gomez is a powerful citizen of this town. He has influence in Austin. I'd lose my star if this thing backfired."

Roy's eyes studied Tommy Stockton intently. "Not afraid of smelling a little gunpowder, Tommy?" he asked. "According to Texanna, you've been eating your heart out to get a line on this counterfeiting business."

Tommy Stockton flushed to the roots of his hair.

"Wait here, Roy," the sheriff said. "I'll go round up our little posse, and to heck with what happens. If we find an illegal printing press at the Tres Coronas this morning, Furtado Gomez's influence at the State Capital won't do him a bit of good."

Ten minutes later Tommy Stockton was introducing Roy Rogers to his two deputies, the town marshal, and a pair of husky men wearing the badges of the United States Border Patrol.

"I suggest we do it this way," Roy Rogers said. "Nobody knows me in Gunsight. I'll go into Furtado Gomez's place, and I have a hunch Señor Rattlesnake's smugglers will recognize me very quickly. I have reason to believe they'll think I'm a ghost returned from the dead, and will leave the Tres Coronas in a big hurry."

Tommy Stockton grinned. "And we'll have the place surrounded," the sheriff said. "Okay, men?"

One of the Border Patrolmen grunted enthusiastically. "Uncle Sam's been after that counterfeitin' ring for several years, and nobody ever thought to search Furtado's place," he said. "Only thing that worries me is Roy Rogers going alone."

Roy's grin carried no suggestion of worry.

"If any of you men—known star-toters—were to enter the place, shooting would be sure to start. I don't think I'll be running any great risk."

Roy shook hands all around, got his instructions as to how to locate Furtado Gomez's place in the Mexican quarter, and left the jailhouse. He knew that by the time he was inside the Tres Coronas, Sheriff Stockton and his posse would have all exits under guard.

Leaving the main street, Roy made his way up the south slope of the canyon into the portion of Gunsight known locally as "Chihuahuaville."

He found the quarter to be typically Mexican. The main street was named Cinco De Mayo, like main streets of many towns in Mexico. And the architecture was from south of the Rio.

Adobe hotels were sign-boarded as *posadas;* there were candlemaker's shops, and high-arched arcades overshadowing the sidewalks. Goats and chickens ran loose on the streets; farther up the hill were the *jacal* hovels of the poor who made up the bulk of the Mexican population. Most of them worked the mines farther up-canyon.

This was a bit of Old Mexico transplanted into Texas. In spite of the dirt and smells and the swarms of black-eyed, half-naked children running underfoot, it was a place of romance and drama.

Strolling leisurely along the arcades, past fat Mexican women shopping for their Sunday dinner at the market places, Roy gave little hint of the desperate mission that had brought him here. He appeared to be another gringo tourist out sightseeing, perhaps shopping for tortillas or bright-painted gourds or Mexican pottery.

Thus he came to Furtado Gomez's place—an adobe building with three crowns painted on its front, the Tres Coronas, meeting-place of Señor Rattlesnake's smugglers.

Loosening his six-guns in holsters, Roy Rogers shouldered through the batwing doors into the smoky stench of the barroom.

As Sheriff Stockton had predicted, the place was jammed with Mexican miners making merry.

For a moment Roy Rogers stood just inside the doorway, peering through the smoke-filled room. Then his gaze came to rest on a circular gambling table where a dozen Mexicans were playing monte, using gold coins for chips.

Five of those Mexicans Roy recognized instantly as the men he had seen in Señor Rattlesnake's den south of the Rio last night. Pedro wore a bandage over the knot on his skull. In the game with him were Heraclio and Flores, Gonzales and Pablo.

Strolling over to that table, Roy tapped Pedro on the shoulder and drawled in the softest of voices, "Gambling away Señor Rattlesnake's smuggling wages so soon, *amigo?*"

CHAPTER XIII

The effect of Roy's words on Pedro was little short of amazing.

Eyes bulging from their sockets, the Mexican miner kicked back his chair, leveled a trembling finger at the gringo cowboy and shrieked in a voice which brought an instant hush to the hubbub of sound in the saloon.

"You are *muerte*—a dead man!" he cried. "You were hanged last night! You have come from the grave to haunt us!"

Recoiling from Roy as if the cowboy were a coiled snake, Pedro plunged off into the crowd, yelling like a crazy man.

Four other Mexicans at Pedro's table were similarly effected by sight of Roy Rogers. Upsetting the monte layout with a scatter of chiming gold coins, four men answering to the names of Flores, Gonzales, Heraclio and Pablo scrambled off in Pedro's wake, yelling at the top of their lungs.

An instant later the five peons who thought they had seen the ghost of a lynch victim raced out through a side door into an alley flanking the Tres

128

Coronas. Waiting for them there were Sheriff Tommy Stockton and a Border Patrol inspector.

Roy Rogers smiled as he saw the mad scramble for the spilled gold on the floor of the barroom. The other Mexicans in this place believed that Roy had frightened a quintet of drunken men, and were all laughing uproariously.

One of them, a pot-bellied man with dark complexion dressed in a gaudy *charro* costume heavy with gold braid and red velvet, came from behind the bar and bowed ceremoniously to Roy.

"Welcome, *Señor Rangero,*" this man said in oily Spanish. "What brings a gringo lawman to my humble place of business?"

Roy brushed a hand across Whetlaw's silver star.

"A friendly little call, señor," Rogers said, still smiling innocently. "Could you introduce me to Señor Furtado Gomez?"

For an instant Roy thought he saw fear flash in the man's shoe-button eyes.

Bowing from the waist, the bartender said, "I am Furtado, *Señor Rangero.* Surely you seek no one who patronizes the Tres Coronas. We have no fights here, no trouble."

Roy grinned disarmingly. "Of course. Your place is the most respectable in Chihuahuaville, I am sure. Could we speak a moment in private?"

Bowing and scraping, Furtado Gomez cleared a

path for his Texas Ranger guest. He led Roy Rogers
to a door marked *Privado—No Entrada*.

When Furtado Gomez had closed the door on the
babble of sound, he turned to his guest with the
oiliest of grins.

"Be seated," he said in English. "Whom do you
seek? Surely I have no evil-doer under my roof."

Gomez jumped back as he found himself staring
into the muzzles of Roy Rogers's matched six-guns.

"I want *you*, Señor Gomez," Roy said, his voice
icy with menace. "The charge is printing counterfeit money."

"You joke, *Señor Rangero*. I am a poor bartender.
What do I know of preenting *dinero?*"

Roy thumbed his Colt .45's to full cock.

"Five of your patrons brought bundles of Chinese
rice paper to this place before dawn today," Roy
said. "Señor Rattlesnake receives your money for
this contraband. Your five smugglers, your go-be-
tweens, even now are under arrest. You saw them in
a hurry to leave your saloon?"

Terror flickered in the depths of Furtado Gomez's
ink-black eyes. Then he regained his composure.

"Eet ees a lie, *Señor Rangero*. I know nothing of
Señor Rattlesnake. You cannot prove these lies
which some enemy of mine has put in your ears."

Keeping his guns trained on Gomez, knowing the
man was as dangerous as a coiled sidewinder, Roy

"I Want You, Señor Gomez," Said Roy

stepped over to a window and called through it. A moment later Sheriff Tommy Stockton was crawling into Furtado's private office.

"Those miners have all confessed to being runners between Señor Rattlesnake and Furtado Gomez, Roy." The sheriff chuckled. "They think you're a sure-enough ghost. I've got the marshal locking them up in my calaboose now."

Roy Rogers assumed his most blood-thirsty scowl. Turning to the trembling barkeeper, he said, "I will give you exactly five seconds to show us where you print that counterfeit money, Señor Gomez, before I fill you full of lead. Start talking."

Feeling his world collapsing about him, Furtado Gomez lost all semblance of defiance.

Stooping, he rolled back a colorful Navajo rug on the floor, to reveal the square shape of a trap door.

Sheriff Stockton leaped forward to seize the iron ringbolt which the rug had concealed. Lifting the trap, he looked down into a cellar. In the semi-darkness of that underground room, he saw a printing press, drums of ink, and other equipment.

Standing up, Stockton whipped a pair of hand-cuffs from a pocket of his bullhide chaps, and snapped them on Gomez's wrists.

The whistle of a mining company's railroad loco-motive on a side track behind Tommy Stockton's cottage roused Roy Rogers from a sound sleep in the sheriff's bed. Peering out the window, he saw Gunsight bathed in the red glow of sundown. He had slept out the entire day like a drugged man.

Greatly refreshed, Roy was thinking now of supper. Stepping out of Stockton's home, he caught sight of a familiar group of riders in front of the jail door. All were from Box C ranch—Buck Conroy and his daughter, and Jingo Bates, the blind foreman. With them were pack horses laden with supplies for Mystery Rancho.

At sight of Roy Rogers, old Buck Conroy's face broke into a welcoming grin. Texanna stepped down from her pinto and ran toward Rogers.

"Tommy told us how you captured that counterfeiter gang this morning," the girl said, gripping Roy's hands hard. "It's so wonderful—the first break of good news we've had in years."

Buck Conroy joined his daughter and shook Roy's hand.

"Tommy says you've got a line on Señor Rattlesnake," the Box C rancher said. "I'm hoping that with him out of the way, the Ghost of Mystery Rancho will be disposed of at the same time. I believe they are one and the same man."

Roy scowled in the sheriff's direction, regretting that Tommy Stockton had given his future father-in-law so much information.

It was on the tip of his tongue to let Conroy know that he was mistaken, that the Ghost was most likely someone on his own ranch. But he kept silent, realizing it was not impossible that Conroy himself might be the Ghost.

"The Ghost believes I am dead," Roy said. "I think it would be just as well if you returned to Box C with the news that I *am* dead."

Texanna laughed. "Roy Rogers is dead," she said. "All right—that means you won't come back home with us then?"

Sheriff Stockton and Jingo Bates joined them in the tight little group.

"I'd like to hide out somewhere in Tomahawk Basin for the next few days, Sheriff," Roy said. "I want to spy on any further activities the Ghost may make, thinking I am out of the way."

Buck Conroy grunted. "I hope," the old rancher said, "that in your scouting rides around my ranch, you run across my Chinese cook. He didn't show up all day. He was a good cook, too. I'd hate to lose him."

Roy Rogers gave no sign of the effect this news had on him. Fung Ling missing? That could mean that the Chinese had taken Roy's advice and had escaped from Mystery Rancho. It could also mean that Fung Ling had run into trouble.

"If you're lookin' for a place to hide out," Jingo Bates spoke up, "how about our line-camp cabin in

Skeleton Canyon, boss? We got a good supply of grub stashed there, and there's plenty of water and feed for Roy's horse."

Conroy glanced around at his blind foreman.

"An excellent suggestion, Jingo," the old Texan said. Turning to Roy, Conroy continued, "this line-camp cabin is in an isolated section of my range, Roy. No one ever visits it."

Roy listened closely while Jingo Bates gave him directions on how to reach Skeleton Canyon, which was on the west side of the Basin, in the foothills of the Navajada range.

"We ought to arrange some method of getting any important news to you there, Roy," spoke up Sheriff Stockton.

Texanna said quickly, "I know—Bronc Alamar's little niece, Pepita. Her father is one of our *vaqueros*, Roy. She rides all over the Basin, and would attract no suspicions. If we need to send you any messages, Pepita can be our courier. She's a little girl of nine, and we can trust her to hold her tongue."

Roy scowled, not too sure he liked this arrangement, but aware that the occasion might arise when Box C might want to communicate with him.

"All right," he said. "I'll make my headquarters at Skeleton Canyon line camp. Remember—spread the word that I'm dead."

CHAPTER XIV

Box C's line-camp cabin in Skeleton Canyon was an adobe structure with maguay-leaf shingles, windows which long since had lost their glass, and four bunks covered with moldy straw ticks. There was a rusty cookstove in one corner, and a plentiful stock of canned food, dried meat, beans, coffee, and sugar.

In more prosperous days, before the Ghost had stripped Box C of its cowboy crew, this camp had been the headquarters of Conroy's men during round-up time on the west slopes of Tomahawk Basin. But it was obvious that no one had lived here for several years.

There was a bubbling cold spring outside the cabin, with a natural meadow of lush bluestem grass where Trigger could graze. Behind the cabin was the steep, rocky slope of Skeleton Canyon's south flank; opposite lifted the stone face of a cliff. From the front door Roy could command a wide view of Tomahawk Basin.

His first day of hiding out Roy Rogers spent on a rocky pinnacle of the Navajadas, from which lookout post he could study the quicksand bog and

136

Señor Rattlesnake's secret tunnel exit through the field glasses which he always carried.

He could also keep watch on the ruins of Haunted Mission on the northern skyline; and the powerful glasses let him know what was going on at Box C.

It was even possible for him to make out Gunsight's cluster of buildings, ten miles across the Basin to eastward. All in all, Roy had a bird's-eye view of everything that happened on Mystery Rancho.

It was Roy's plan to spy on any smuggler activity in the region of the Rio Grande tunnel, with an eye to finding out what man power Señor Rattlesnake commanded. This would guide him in choosing a posse which he and Sheriff Stockton would, in the near future, lead through the tunnel under the Rio Grande.

The first long day proved uneventful, however. Through the glasses he saw Texanna out riding on the Basin floor, accompanied by the persistent though unwelcome Jingo Bates.

When nightfall put an end to his vigil, Roy returned to the line-camp cabin.

It was while he was preparing supper that Roy thought he saw something unusual in this cabin, some tiny detail which was different from what it was when he had left the place that morning.

He could not be sure what had roused his curiosity; plumb his memory of this single-roomed hut as he would, he was unable to trace the uncomfortable feeling he had that someone had paid this cabin a visit during the day.

Finally, after he had eaten his supper and had washed the tin dishes, Roy believed he knew what was bothering him.

He had spread his blankets on one of the four bunks. Under that bunk were a number of wooden boxes filled with canned food. Something told him that the position of those boxes had been changed ever so slightly.

"My imagination's working over time," Roy told himself aloud.

Nevertheless, he crossed the room with the lantern and squatted down to inspect the boxes of food.

Upon his arrival in Skeleton Canyon, Roy had given the rammed earth floor of this cabin a thorough sweeping. Looking closely at the boxes under his bunk, Roy saw where the rectangular outline in the dust indicated that the boxes had been shifted from their original positions.

He had dragged the boxes out from under the bunk to inspect their contents shortly after reaching the Box C camp, but he had not moved them since he had swept the floor. Yet the dust had been disturbed here during his absence.

Every nerve tingling with suspense, Roy started removing the cans of evaporated milk which one of the boxes contained, knowing that there was a risk of touching off a trap of some kind.

As soon as he had removed the first layer of milk cans, his suspicions were confirmed.

Under those cans had been placed a large bundle of round, sticklike objects wrapped in greasy yellow paper.

"Dynamite!" Roy whispered, lifting the bundle out of the box after first making sure that no trigger arrangement was attached to them. "These explosives weren't here this morning."

Strangely enough, none of the sticks of dynamite had a percussion cap or fuse attached.

But under the first bundle of explosives was a shoe-box sized container of cardboard. Lifting the lid, Roy shuddered. The box was filled to the brim with shiny copper tubes resembling cartridge cases.

"Dynamite percussion caps," Roy muttered. "A hard enough jolt would touch them off. Enough to detonate the explosive and blow this cabin to bits, and me with it!"

Someone had planted this makeshift bomb under his bed for a deliberate purpose, he knew. The fact that this bunk was the only one of the four which had been covered with blankets had tipped off the unknown intruder as to where Roy Rogers planned to sleep.

A bullet fired into that box would do the trick

easily enough, Roy thought. *The impact of a rifle slug would be more than enough to explode the percussion caps, and they would set off the dynamite sticks on top.*

Roy twisted around to size up the room. Directly across the cabin from his bed was a three-foot-square window, covered only by a rotten gunny sack.

Crossing the room, leaving his lantern behind, Roy squinted through a rip in the soggy burlap. He had a view of the south slope of Skeleton Canyon. Any ambusher crouched up that slope could draw a bead on this window with a rifle. If he had planned his angle of fire carefully in advance, a marksman could put a bullet into the box of dynamite under Roy's bunk the first shot.

Rogers ticked off the persons who knew he was hiding out here in Skeleton Canyon, trying to decide which of them might have engineered this fiendish thing.

"Buck Conroy—I don't see what he would stand to gain by putting me out of the way, knowing I've come here to track down the Ghost who is running Box C into bankruptcy.

"Texanna knows I'm camping here. But this is too brutal a thing for a woman to have thought up.

"Jingo Bates? A blind man could have planted the dynamite here, but he could hardly fire a rifle accurately enough to lay his shot through that window at the proper angle."

That left only Tommy Stockton, the sheriff of Gunsight. A keen judge of human nature, Roy did not see where Texanna's intended husband could be the guilty party.

But what if someone had talked at Box C? What if Bronc Alamar, for instance, found out that Rogers wasn't dead, as Roy had carefully coached his Box C friends to report when they got home?

Returning to the lantern he had left on the floor by the bunk, Roy unscrewed the cap in the fuel tank and carefully poured out all the coal oil it contained, leaving only the wick moist. He estimated that the lamp would go out inside of ten minutes, when the flame exhausted the oil in its wick.

Placing the lantern on a table near the window, Roy went to another window at a darkened corner of the line-camp shack and crawled out into the night.

The moon had not yet risen and the feeble shine of the Texas stars did not penetrate Skeleton Canyon.

Wetting a finger to test the direction of the wind, Roy Rogers made a wide circuit of the meadow where Trigger was grazing. He did not want his horse to catch his scent on the breeze and betray him with a whickered greeting.

Reaching the south wall of the canyon, above

the cabin, Roy squatted down behind a thicket of prickly pear cactus and settled down to wait for whatever might develop. He kept his attention fixed on the square of yellow light where the lantern illuminated the burlap-covered window.

Some ten minutes later the light flickered and went out, leaving the cabin in total darkness.

The whitewashed adobe walls of the shack were plainly visible in the starlight, however, with the door and window openings making black, easily seen targets in the night.

If hostile eyes were watching the Box C cabin from the rimrock above, their owner would assume that Roy Rogers had blown out his light and gone to bed.

Before the hour was out, the moon rose and sent its silvery witch-glow into the rock-ribbed notch of Skeleton Canyon, throwing details into bold relief.

Suddenly, to his ears came a harsh whisper of sound, somewhere up the slope and to his left. A tiny rain of pebbles made a miniature avalanche as something—a prowling coyote, perhaps, or a human being—moved down the steep canyon slope.

Cocking his .45's, Roy Rogers waited, keening the night with ears and eyes for a repetition of that alien sound.

It came again—the unmistakable scrape of a spur rowel on a lava rock. No coyote or armadillo was scuttling through the brush up there!

A deep quiet settled in Skeleton Canyon, making Roy wonder if the sound of his own pounding heart was loud enough to reach that invisible prowler.

Somewhere far off, a coyote barked at the moon. An owl winged overhead, made its swooping arrow-straight dive to the grassy meadow and locked its talons on a foraging field mouse.

Then, an eternity later, Roy's sharp eyes detected a movement along the slope some fifty feet west of where he crouched behind the cactus clump.

Focusing his eyes on that shadow, Roy saw the glint of moonlight on a Winchester barrel.

The prowler was angling down the slope directly toward Roy. Some thirty feet away the man halted, kneeling behind a large bubble-pitted boulder of pink volcanic rock.

The rifle-toter was close enough for Roy to see that he was wearing one of Box C's scarlet shirts with white crescents stitched on the pockets.

As he watched, Roy saw the man rest his .30-30 barrel on the rock, taking careful aim at the black square of the window of the cabin.

Roy came to his feet, realizing he would gain nothing by letting this man send a slug into the box of explosive and destroy the line-camp cabin.

Without warning, Rogers triggered a Colt. His bullet struck the lava boulder where the man was crouching with rifle stock cuddled to cheek, and ricocheted off into space with a screaming sound like a plucked harp string.

The rifleman leaped to his feet and whirled about, the moonlight flashing on his bared teeth.

"Bronc Alamar!" Rogers shouted, as he recognized the face of the Box C cavvy wrangler. "I sort of thought it would be you, trying to blast me to glory."

Bronc Alamar was crouched like a gorilla beside the rock, his Winchester sliding off the boulder into the tumbleweeds beyond.

The wrangler's surly gaze was fixed on the Texas Ranger star shining on Roy's shirt. The man seemed completely paralyzed by the shock of finding his intended victim out here in the open instead of asleep inside the cabin.

"Get your hands up," Roy snarled, "or I'll ventilate your ribs with some hot lead, Bronc. I'm in no mood to b—"

At that instant a rifle's deafening report blasted from the rim of the north cliff beyond the cabin. Roy felt the air-whip of a steel-jacketed slug fan his nose, as the slug smashed into the rocks beside him, shedding its smoking jacket on the rubble.

With a wild yell of panic, Bronc Alamar turned and started running in zigzag fashion up the south slope. Roy's guns blazed, but the bullets with which he had intended to cripple the wrangler missed in

A Bullet Whipped Past Roy

the tricky moonlight.

The rifle on the north rim blasted again, its echoes clamoring wildly up Skeleton Canyon. This time Roy felt the jerk of the slug drilling his Stetson, and he knew that Alamar's partner had his range.

Flinging himself to the ground, Roy slithered his way toward the shelter of the boulder where Alamar had rested his rifle.

The Winchester on the north rimrock was beating up echoes again, a steady string of fast-triggered shots from a repeater.

Bullets were trailing Roy Rogers across the ground, spraying sand in his eyes, peppering the ground behind and above him.

Through the tail of his eye the cowboy saw Bronc Alamar dive into a split in the canyon wall, out of sight.

The rifle, having emptied its magazine, went silent on the north rim. In the following quiet, Roy got to his feet and made it safely to the boulder which would protect him from the other outlaw's rifle fire.

Echoes of the gun's fusillade were fading in the far recesses of the canyon. Closer at hand, Roy could hear the scrambling passage of Bronc Alamar as the scarlet-shirted cavvy wrangler climbed the eroded gully toward the summit.

Roy groaned, knowing that he could not expose

himself now to pursue Alamar without drawing the deadly fire of the wrangler's sidekick on the other side of the canyon.

A shift in the wind brought to his ears the sound of a rifle's lever cranking a cartridge into the breech of the .30-30. That meant the other foe had reloaded his magazine and was waiting for Roy to show himself.

Minutes later, Roy saw Bronc Alamar's remote shape on the skyline as he reached the ridge and vanished beyond it. Alamar was not lingering to make a gun fight of it.

A gloomy quiet settled down. Knowing he was watched from the north rimrock, Roy concentrated his gaze in that direction, hoping to glimpse the man with the Winchester moving to another location. But even if he spotted his attacker, Roy knew the man was out of six-gun range.

Much later Roy heard a muffled sound of hoofbeats and knew that Bronc Alamar was riding away from the shoulder of the canyon. But he dared not leave the boulder's protection, with the Winchester covering this ground.

And so Roy Rogers spent the remainder of the night, cold and shivering, watching for a target which never presented itself. When dawn's first blood-red light penetrated the blue haze of Skeleton Canyon, Roy took his chance and stood up.

His appearance drew no shot from any direction. Apparently the Winchester toter who had covered Alamar's approach to the line-camp cabin had withdrawn some time during the night.

After a hasty breakfast, Roy Rogers emerged from the cabin carrying the dynamite bundles and box of detonating caps—the latter well cushioned against shock in a rolled-up blanket.

He loaded his dangerous cargo in a gunny sack and, after saddling Trigger, tied the sack behind his cantle.

Rogers had thought up a very practical use for Bronc Alamar's dynamite. The first project to come after his raid on Señor Rattlesnake's smuggler den across the Rio would be to blast the under-river tunnel, flooding it and ending forever this secret entry from Chihuahua into Texas.

By noon Roy had arrived at the brushy draw near the quicksand bog. He carefully concealed the sack of explosives in this brush, and then left the draw to have a look at the *sumidero*. He saw no evidence that the gangplank had been trundled out of the cavern in the last day or so.

His next move remained to be decided upon. Should he go directly to Gunsight and arrange with Sheriff Stockton and the Border Patrol inspectors for the raid on Señor Rattlesnake's den? Or should he head for Box C and arrest Bronc Alamar for his would-be murder attempt in Skeleton Canyon last night?

After some debate with himself, Roy decided on the latter course. Whether Bronc Alamar was the Ghost—or whether he had attempted to dynamite Roy because of his personal hatred stemming from the Fung Ling episode in the bunkhouse—Roy had evidence enough against the wrangler to jail him.

Midway across Tomahawk Basin on his way to Conroy's ranch, Roy Rogers caught sight of a lone rider heading westward toward Skeleton Canyon. Sighting his field glasses on that rider, Roy saw that it was a small Mexican girl on a buckskin pony.

"That'll be Pepita," Roy mused. "Carrying a message to me. That could either be from Texanna or the sheriff."

Knowing the message must be urgent, Roy swung off the Box C road and put Trigger toward Skeleton Canyon. By the time he arrived there two hours later, little Pepita had come and gone; but he found an envelope thrust in a knothole of the cabin door.

Opening it, Roy Rogers read:

Roy:

I have urgent news from Tommy Stockton. Meet me as soon as possible at the Haunted Mission. I'll wait for you there until sundown. I can't put the news in writing.

Texanna Conroy

CHAPTER XV

THE WELL OF BONES

Texanna Conroy was pacing nervously back and forth along the wall of the ancient chapel built by the Spanish padres centuries before, when she saw Roy Rogers approaching on Trigger from the ridge beyond High Gate.

Relief shone in the girl's amber eyes as she saw the flash of sunlight on Roy's Ranger badge. She had been waiting here at Haunted Mission for more than three hours.

She had left her pinto on picket at the cemetery. She was tempted to ride out to meet Roy, but instead she made her way to the doorway of the mission.

A few feet inside that doorway was the headless skeleton holding two rusty revolvers on its bony knees—the Talking Skull itself was still lying on the mission floor.

A few minutes later Roy Rogers spurred up the ridge, dismounted to leave Trigger ground-hitched at the graveyard along with Texanna's horse, and came toward her at a swift walk.

"Howdy," Roy panted, lifting his Stetson. "I came as soon as I got the message Pepita carried out to the line camp, Texanna. What's wrong?"

Texanna's mouth opened in surprise and her eyes grew big as she heard Roy's words.

"Message? I sent no message, Roy!" the girl cried. "I rode out here in answer to *your* note."

Roy's jaw tightened.

"We've been baited into a trap, Texanna," the cowboy said. "I didn't send you any note. We—"

Texanna removed a sheet of paper from the crescent-rimmed pocket of her scarlet rodeo shirt and handed it to Roy. His eyes shuttled over the printed words:

Texanna:

I must see you at once. Meet me at Haunted Mission. Don't tell anyone about this.

> *Roy Rogers*

Roy dropped the forged note and grabbed Texanna's hand.

"Come on!" he said sharply. "We're getting out of here. This is a trap, with each of us used as bait for the other. We—"

Roy Rogers broke off as he saw a tall figure leap suddenly into the doorway behind the girl and thrust a cocked six-gun against Texanna's back.

It was the Ghost of Mystery Rancho, his snake-like eyes glittering triumphantly behind his skull mask.

"Throw up your arms, *Señor Rangero*," the outlaw ordered in crisp Spanish, "or the *señorita* dies!"

Roy let go his grip on Texanna's hand. He stared at the Ghost, knowing another instant's hesitation would mean a bullet in the girl's spine.

Slowly Roy raised his arms to the level of his Stetson brim. Texanna remained in a frozen posture, terror paralyzing her.

"You were sharp to spot that dynamite in the cabin last night, Señor," leered the Ghost. "You could have lost your life instead of a night's sleep."

Making certain that Texanna was unarmed, the Ghost stepped around from behind the cowgirl and stalked over to where Roy stood. Keeping his gun trained on the cowboy's Ranger star, the Ghost reached out to lift Roy's .45's from holsters and tossed them into a thicket of tumbleweeds beside the mission door.

Then, without warning, the Ghost brought the muzzle of his gun up to smash Roy on the point of the chin.

Knocked senseless, the cowboy slumped in his tracks.

A scream left Texanna's lips as she charged at the skeleton-suited outlaw, ignoring the menace of his gun. The Ghost laughed harshly as the girl clawed at his mask, lifting his gun like a club. Before Texanna could dodge, the Ghost clubbed the girl across the head, wilting her alongside Roy Rogers.

Moving without haste, the Ghost stepped back into the Haunted Mission, and emerged a moment later with two coils of lariat rope.

Kneeling between his unconscious victims, the Ghost tied Roy's arms tightly at the wrists, then pinioned his arms to his sides from elbow to shoulders.

That done, the skull-masked outlaw trussed up Texanna in similar fashion, using the other rope.

The Ghost then walked around the corner of the bell tower and into the near-by chaparral. His horse was picketed there, a leggy blue roan bearing a Box C brand. He unlooped a canvas waterbag from the saddle horn and returned to where Roy and Texanna lay.

Dousing the cool water over the heads of his victims, the Ghost of Mystery Rancho waited until Roy Rogers and the girl had regained consciousness. Then he lifted them by the armpits and hauled them to their feet, one after the other.

"Señor Rogers," the Ghost said, his voice sounding oddly distant in Roy's ears, "you came to this very spot last week with Ranger John Whetlaw, whose badge you are now wearing. You are curious to know what happened to the four lawmen who vanished without trace upon arriving at Mystery Rancho. Come with me. I'll show you the answer to that riddle."

Roy Rogers felt his spine turn into an icicle. He was remembering what he had heard Señor Rattlesnake say the other night at the hangtree on the Gunsight road. The Ghost's victims had been hurled into a place he called the Well of Bones.

With the Ghost prodding them from behind, the two prisoners walked into the interior of the Haunted Mission and out a back exit facing on the brushy hillslope.

There was no path or visible break in the thorny thickets, but the Ghost steered them past a yellow-flowering *agarita* clump and on into the heart of the shadowy jungle of mesquites.

A dozen yards inside these brambles, out of sight of the mission's crumbling ruins, Roy saw a weather-beaten door built into an outcrop of quartz.

Going ahead of them, the Ghost opened the door to reveal a tunnel similar to a prospector's test hole, chiseled into the heart of the mountainside.

"This cavern," the Ghost explained, "was built in secret by the Spanish padres of long ago. It gave them a passage of escape in case of Indian attack."

From a rocky niche just inside the door, the Ghost of Mystery Rancho took a stub of candle. He lighted it, and beckoned Roy and the girl to pass him on their way into the padres' getaway tunnel.

Moving like sleepwalkers in the grip of a horrid nightmare, the two prisoners headed into the tunnel.

The Ghost brought up the rear, his candle showing them the jagged rock walls and ceiling of the passage.

The tunnel made a right-angle turn some fifty feet from the entrance, and Roy saw blazing sunlight at the tunnel's outlet a short distance away.

A moment later he and Texanna stepped out into the sun's hot glare, to find themselves in the pit of a narrow canyon.

To their right were the tumble-down remains of an ancient barn, built by the Spaniards to shelter their stock. The loft of this barn was filled with hay.

Everything about this place brooded mystery and menace. The spell of it brought a choked sob to Texanna's lips, put a prickle of apprehension on the nape of Roy's neck.

"The old padres who built the mission overlooking Tomahawk Basin didn't have a supply of water here," the Ghost was saying, as he blew out his stub of candle. "So they used a glacial pothole beyond the barn there as a cistern to catch rain water. It so happens the cistern is dry now, because Texas has had a drought. I think you will be interested in seeing what that cistern contains."

Helpless before the threat of the Ghost's leveled gun, Roy Rogers and Texanna Conroy rounded the corner of the barn and came in sight of a roughly circular hole in the bedrock floor of the canyon.

Some prehistoric waterfall had probably worn out

that deep bowllike hole in the rock. A pole and rawhide ladder slanted down into the cistern, and over it was a crude windlass hoist consisting of a crossbeam between supporting rocks, which the Spanish priests had used for lifting water out of the cistern.

Roy could not stifle a groan of despair as he reached the top of that ladder and looked down at the most gruesome sight his eyes had ever beheld.

Twenty feet below the overhanging rim of the cistern, the rocky bottom of the pothole was littered with bones—human bones, the skeletons of men who had been hurled to their dooms there.

And there was another dead man at the bottom of the ladder, a murder victim so recently dead that the body was still covered with a black silk garment.

"Fung Ling!" gasped Roy Rogers, as he recognized the corpse of Buck Conroy's Chinese cook. "Then this is the Well of Bones!"

The Ghost was pushing Texanna toward the ladder. As Roy Rogers stared, he saw the masked outlaw assist the girl to put her booted feet on one of the rungs and start her descent into the Well of Bones, working her way slowly and clumsily because her arms were tied to her sides.

Roy thought, "The Ghost isn't going to throw us down there to be killed instantly—he's leaving us there to starve!"

When Texanna was almost to the bottom of the

ladder, the Ghost turned to Roy Rogers and motioned with his gun for the cowboy to follow.

Roy was tempted to hurl himself at the Ghost, inviting a merciful bullet. But that would be to leave Texanna alone here, with no one to share her last agonizing days before thirst and hunger ended her suffering.

Mouth locked grimly, Roy got his feet on the ladder rungs and started down into the padres' cistern. When he finally reached the bottom, he had to jump off the ladder to avoid stepping on Fung Ling's stiffened form.

Even as he regained his balance, Roy had to duck to avoid being struck by the ladder as the Ghost of Mystery Rancho hauled it up.

Texanna, quivering with horror, put her shoulder against Roy's as the two prisoners stared up at the disk of blue sky beyond the cistern's rim, twenty feet overhead. They saw the ladder vanish from sight as the Ghost pulled it from the hole.

Then the Ghost's skull-masked head appeared overhead, to send his last taunting words at the doomed pair.

"No one alive except myself knows of the existence of this place or the tunnel that leads to it, *amigos*. You're in good company down there. Look around at the skeletons of the star-toters who came before you, Ranger Rogers!"

CHAPTER XVI

LIVING DEATH

For long minutes after the Ghost of Mystery Rancho had disappeared, Roy Rogers stood sizing up the pothole. He came to the conclusion that escape was utterly impossible.

Even if their arms were not bound, the beetling walls of the pothole were as slick as glass, completely without toeholds anywhere.

He stared at the corpse of Fung Ling, dead with a bullet in the brain, and a great sadness swept through him. The old Chinese had been murdered for his ruse at the hangman's tree the other night. Somehow the Ghost had found out that his Oriental interpreter had double-crossed him.

Hearing the soft sobbing of Texanna, who stood leaning against him, Roy said huskily, "Don't worry, Texanna. As long as we're alive, there's hope for us. Maybe someone saw you riding out to Haunted Mission this morning—perhaps your father will search for you. If we could yell loud enough, our voices might carry to the mission."

Texanna shook her head despairingly.

"No, Roy," she said, controlling herself with an effort. "There is no hope of rescue. The note I found on the window sill of my bedroom this morning—it said to let no one know I was riding to see you. I—I thought the note was genuine, that you had visited Box C during the night and left it on my window."

Roy grinned with an assurance he was far from feeling.

"But just the same, someone might have seen you leaving Box C. And if your horse shows up at the corral tonight without a rider, your father will search the Basin with a fine-tooth comb."

But Texanna was inconsolable.

"No—I left before Dad was awake, before Jingo and the others had left the bunkhouse. No one saw me leave. And as for my paint getting back home—you know the Ghost will shoot my horse—and Trigger."

Roy shuddered, realizing the truth of the girl's words. The thought of having his faithful palomino dropped by the Ghost's bullet, out there in front of the Haunted Mission, put a stab of anger and remorse through the cowboy. To Roy Rogers, Trigger was "folks."

Roy insisted that Texanna seat herself to rest on a boulder which had broken off the mountainside above the canyon and rolled into the Well of Bones.

He looked around at the whitened human bones which buzzards had scattered over the rocky floor of the pothole.

A grim story was written in those bleached remains. There was a grinning human skull with a pair of thick-lensed spectacles still in place over the hollow eyesockets. Over yonder was a latticework of ribs still intact, with bits of decayed fabric from the wearer's shirt hanging in tatters over the bones. Still pinned to the rotted cloth was a tarnished badge identical to the one Roy had received from John Whetlaw a few days ago—the circle-enclosed five-pointed star of a Texas Ranger.

Roy's searching eyes located two more law badges amid the skulls and débris—the shields of the United States Border Patrol. He found another Texas Ranger star, and still another badge with the words *U.S. Marshal* still legible on it.

Here, then, was the answer to the mystery which had confounded John Whetlaw. The lawmen who, sent to Tomahawk Basin to solve the mystery of the Ghost, had died here in the Well of Bones.

Texanna broke the silence, her voice echoing hollowly off the enclosing rock wall. "To think I'll never see my beloved Tommy again—or Daddy—they'll never know what happened to us."

Try as he might, Roy Rogers could think of nothing to say to console the girl.

He tried to loosen his arms in their bonds, but the flesh was beginning to swell for the Ghost had tied his knots with devilish tightness.

A few minutes later the blinding disk of the sun came in view over the pothole's rim, and Roy knew they faced a new discomfort. During the hour or two the sun would pour its punishing heat into this pothole, the granite walls of the hole would radiate heat like the sides of a red-hot stove.

A dazzling spear of reflected sunlight blinded Roy as he paced around the bone-littered floor of their prison. It was the reflection of the Texas sun off the thick lenses of the eye-glasses which one of the skulls wore.

Roy turned back to Texanna. The girl had recovered her self-control now, and she managed a wry grin as he faced her.

"You know," she said, "I wish the Ghost had relieved my girlish curiosity enough to unmask before us. I haven't the slightest idea whose face is behind that mask."

To make conversation and get the girl's mind off their approaching doom, Roy Rogers told her the story of Bronc Alamar's attack in Skeleton Canyon last night.

"So you think Bronc is the Ghost," she said. "I don't doubt it, at that. He's always missing from the ranch and never explains where he's been."

Roy averted his head to avoid another blinding flash of sunlight off the skull's eye-glasses. Finally giving way to a fit of annoyance, he stepped over to the skull and rolled it over with his boot toe, knocking the spectacles off.

Lifting a boot, Roy smashed one of the lenses with his heel.

Then, staring down at the little sparkling pile of crushed glass, an idea exploded in his brain.

"Texanna," he said, his voice trembling with excitement, "I think we have a chance. Wait—"

Texanna Conroy stared fearfully at the young cowboy as she saw him stretch out full length on the rocky floor, alongside the skull and the pair of spectacles he had partially destroyed. The dismaying thought came to the girl in that moment that Roy Rogers's brain had snapped under the strain.

The feeling grew as she saw that Roy was hitching his way closer to the pair of spectacles until he could get his fingers on the corroded gold rim of the lens which was still intact.

Then, holding the spectacles, Roy heaved himself to his feet and came over to where Texanna sat on the boulder.

"This lens will make a burning glass as long as the sun is visible down here," Roy said. "Turn around and hold still. I think I can sever your bonds—"

Texanna got the idea then, and a wild burst of hope came to her. She stood up, carefully edging herself around closer to the white cone of light which the sun's rays made as they passed through the

Roy Used the Lens as a Burning Glass

thick concave-convex lens.

"But even if you burn this lariat through," the girl found herself saying, "how—what good will that do us?"

Roy shrugged, wriggling his hand around until the focal point of the lens's concentrated rays rested on one of Texanna's ropes.

"I haven't thought that far ahead yet," he panted. "But we'll be a lot more comfortable, free of these ropes. By the time the sun comes around tomorrow, our flesh will have swollen over our ropes—"

It was difficult work focusing the rays of the spectacle lens on the rope. It called for rock-steady nerves on both their parts. But within minutes after Roy got the pinpoint of light converging on the rawhide, a wisp of smoke spiraled up.

Minutes dragged like an eternity. From time to time they had to shift position, as the sun moved on its timeless arc across the patch of sky visible from the Well of Bones.

At times, when Roy's hand trembled involuntarily and sent the hot point of the light rays on Texanna's sleeve, the girl winced from the blistering heat on her skin.

But the burning-glass was doing its work. The rawhide rope was being charred rapidly.

"We've got to do this thing before the sun disappears," Roy said. "This time tomorrow might find us both too weak to stand up."

The interior of the pothole was fast becoming a bake oven. Sweat rinsed their skin, soaked their clothing.

Then, even as the sun's disk touched the rim of the Well of Bones and brought relief from the intolerable heat, Texanna flexed her muscles and the charred rope snapped.

Going down on his knees, Roy got his teeth on the severed lariat and pulled. With Texanna jerking her arms to assist him, the pressure of the Ghost's bonds loosened, uncoiled.

Five minutes later her ropes fell free and Texanna was waving her arms in the air with hysteria close to claiming her.

"I see the haft of a bowie knife sticking out of Fung Ling's sleeve yonder," Roy said, gently lowering the skull's spectacles to the boulder. "If you don't mind—it will make it easier than trying to untie my knots with your fingers."

Texanna overcame her revulsion of the dead man and removed Fung Ling's knife from its sheathe up his sleeve.

A moment later Roy was massaging his hands and arms, free to move them as he willed.

"Figured out what we do from here?" Texanna asked.

Roy grinned. "I have," he said. "Get busy unbraiding these lasso ropes, Texanna. We'll need at least forty or fifty feet of rawhide thong to accomplish what I have in mind."

Asking no questions, the girl set to work unraveling the bonds. Roy was doing likewise with the twisted sisal-fiber riata which Texanna had cut with the dead cook's knife.

By the time they had finished, the sunlight was crawling up the north side of the Well of Bones and they were working in welcome shade.

Taking the various strands of unraveled rope, Roy Rogers tied them together securely and then looped them into a neat coil over his left wrist. He estimated that he had at least ninety feet of combined rawhide thong and sisal rope.

Looking around, Roy spotted Fung Ling's knife resting on the boulder where Texanna had placed it. He tied one end of his rope to the hilt of the bowie, and then motioned Texanna to get back out of the way.

Standing to the left of center of the pothole's bottom, Roy started whirling the knife in blurring circles over his head. When he had the whirling weight moving in a vertical plane, he let go and sent the knife hurling straight toward the zenith.

From her position on the far side of the pothole, Texanna saw the knife blade catch the sun's beams as it shot up out of the pothole, trailing after it the rapidly uncoiling loops of rope from Roy's forearm.

At the top of its flight, the knife wavered in mid-air and then fell like a plummet, back into the Well of Bones. But in so doing, it had dropped over the sturdy wooden windlass beam which spanned the padres' cistern, leaving a loop of sturdy rope over the crossarm!

The knife had hardly clattered on the rocky floor when Roy Rogers picked it up and repeated the process. This time the knife was held by the rope, swinging like a pendulum some six feet off the floor of the Well of Bones—but the windlass crossbeam had another double rope looped around it.

Reaching up to catch the knife, Roy began twisting the knotted sisal cord and rawhide thongs until the spirals met under the crossbeam twenty-five feet overhead.

"These riatas were made to hold a thousand-pound steer at the end of a cow pony's dallies," Roy said exultantly. "I don't think it'll break under my weight." He got a good grip on the twisted rope.

Then Roy's feet left the floor of the Well of Bones as he started climbing, his powerful arms going hand-over-hand up the taut rope.

In a matter of moments, Roy's monkey-like climb had carried him above the rim of the pothole.

He saw no sign of the Ghost lingering near the padres' barn.

After a moment's rest, he flashed a grin of reassurance down to Texanna waiting below him, and swung his legs up and over the crossbeam.

The wood was brittle, rotten with age. The windlass log crackled ominously as Roy worked his way toward the stone supports, and he had a bad moment contemplating what would happen if it broke under his weight and plunged him back into the pothole.

He heard Texanna's glad cry of relief as he reached the end of the windlass beam and dropped safely to the bedrock rim of the pothole.

Panting with exertion, his palms bleeding from the friction of the knotted rope he had climbed, Roy Rogers strode over to where the Ghost of Mystery Rancho had left the sturdy rawhide-jointed pole ladder.

A moment later he was sliding the ladder down into the Well of Bones, and Texanna was scaling the rungs with all the speed and agility of a fireman.

Roy reached out to give Texanna a helping hand, pulling her to the safety of the canyon floor.

Embracing the cowboy in an ecstacy of thanksgiving for the deliverance his ingenuity had brought them, Texanna whispered through her sobs, "Thanks to you, Roy, I'll see Daddy and my Tommy again. Oh, thank you, Roy Rogers."

CHAPTER XVII

"YOU'RE UNDER ARREST, GHOST!"

Well aware that danger might still be waiting for them, Texanna and Roy Rogers rounded the corner of the ruined barn and studied the mouth of the near-by tunnel for long moments before venturing into the open.

Their brief ordeal had left them physically spent, but they would not feel completely secure as long as they were near the Haunted Mission.

Without a candle to guide them, they worked their way slowly through the escape passage of the ancient Spaniards until they reached the outer door.

It opened to the pressure of Roy Rogers's shoulder, and once more they waited and rested in the shade of the chaparral, listening for sounds which might indicate that the Ghost of Mystery Rancho was still near by.

Ordering Texanna to remain in the concealing brush, Roy took his chances and headed into the open. A short run brought him inside the Haunted Mission, and he moved through its shadowy gloom until he stood beside the Talking Skull's skeleton, looking through the arched doorway at the far-flung expanse of Tomahawk Basin.

Nothing moved out there. Convinced that the Ghost had departed, Roy stepped outside and swung his gaze toward the cemetery where he and Texanna had left their saddle horses.

Roy's heart sank as he saw no trace of Trigger or the girl's pinto. Had the Ghost led them or driven them away and destroyed them?

He remembered that the Ghost had tossed his six-guns into the tumbleweeds alongside this door and he knew a stab of sweet relief when he found the matched Colts still lying there.

Checking the loads, remembering how his cartridges had been rendered harmless the first night he had spent at Box C, Roy Rogers walked out to the graveyard.

He saw hoofprints leading away from the cemetery, toward the near-by mesquites.

On a hunch, Roy put fingers to teeth and whistled the old signal he had taught Trigger as a colt.

He got an instant response as Trigger whickered from the screening chaparral to westward.

Roy whistled again, but the palomino did not appear.

Scowling, Roy drew his guns and headed into the mesquites. A moment later he saw why Trigger had not answered his call.

Sprawled out in a little clearing there lay the carcass of Texanna's pinto pony, a bullet through its skull. Trigger was standing vigil over the slain horse.

Roy shook his head regretfully, knowing how Texanna had loved the paint. The Ghost had shot this horse to prevent its return to Box C. In all probability the Ghost had tried to shoot Trigger, but the palomino had escaped into the brush.

Leading Trigger away from the slain pinto, Roy mounted and spurred into a gallop, rounding the bell tower of the Haunted Mission and sending his call ahead to Texanna.

The girl emerged from the brush of the mountainside, and as gently as possible Roy broke the news of her pinto's fate.

Texanna took this blow like the thoroughbred she was. As Roy helped her into the saddle, riding double behind the cantle, Texanna whispered, "I— I'd like to see Paint before we go home, Roy. I'll come for him in a buckboard and bury him under the pepper tree down by the windmill where he used to roll as a wobbly-legged foal, six years ago."

After Texanna had seen where the horse was hidden, she returned to where Rogers waited. Dry-eyed, she climbed into saddle and they headed down-slope toward the Basin.

Riding up to Buck Conroy's house an hour later, they found the Box C grounds apparently deserted. Going inside, they found the blind foreman, Jingo

Bates, sitting at his accustomed place on a sofa before the dead fireplace, staring sightlessly into space.

"Where is everybody?" Texanna called out, her voice betraying nothing of the ordeal this day had brought to her and Roy.

Jingo spoke without looking around, "The crew's out on the range hazing in the she-stuff, I guess. Your father and Bronc Alamar went to Gunsight to attend a stock auction at the yards. Beats me why Buck wants to buy any more beef. Before another round-up rolls around, Box C won't be operatin'."

Texanna motioned for Roy to follow her out to the kitchen.

There, out of Jingo's hearing the girl said, "We can forgive Bates for being bitter, Roy. Wait until I change my clothes and I'll whip up a dinner."

When Roy went back outside he saw Jingo Bates heading for the horse barn. By the time Roy reached the same place with Trigger, Jingo had a pony saddled.

"Aim to have myself a canter," the blind foreman said glumly. "One day my memory of the Basin will be gone. All I've got left now is the smell of the sage to enjoy. Why didn't the Ghost kill me that time?"

After Roy had groomed and grained his palomino he returned to the ranch house, where Texanna, her bedraggled hair now combed and brushed to a glossy sheen, was setting a table for two.

"I know you're itching to ride to Gunsight and dab your rope on Bronc Alamar," she said, "but a man has to eat, Roy."

Roy sat down gratefully as Texanna poured him a cup of steaming coffee.

"Tommy Stockton is a lucky man, corraling you for a wife," he said sincerely. "If I succeed in proving that Bronc Alamar is the Ghost, your wedding will take place perty pronto, won't it?"

The girl laughed, busy stirring a kettle of soup on the stove where Fung Ling had prepared Box C's meals ever since she could remember.

"If he has any more excuses to delay the ceremony," she said, "I'll turn him down cold. Anyway, Roy, I'm going to insist that Tommy has you for his best man."

When the meal was finished, Texanna accompanied Roy out to the cavvy corral. No trace of the grief she knew over her pinto's loss was visible as the girl deftly roped a line-back dun out of the Box C remuda and saddled up.

Roy came from the barn with Trigger, and they set forth down the Gunsight road without further delay, the westering sun at their backs.

They reached Gunsight in the blue of dusk, without having met Bronc Alamar and Buck Conroy returning from the auction.

The street was beginning to fill up with workmen

from the mines at this early evening hour, but they saw no trace of the Box C cavvy wrangler.

As they neared the jail building they were caught in the dazzling beam of a locomotive headlight, as a work train from the upper canyon diggings pulled in with its flatcars loaded with muckers. The railroad engine rolled up the dead-end side track which ended behind Tommy Stockton's jail and came to a halt, the miners swarming off the cars.

Going down a black side alley to the hitchrack at the rear of the jail, alongside the panting locomotive, Texanna said in a low voice, "You'll probably find Bronc at the Tres Coronas over in Chihuahuaville, Roy. That's where he has his fun when he comes to town."

Roy shook his head as they hitched up in the darkness.

"I don't think Bronc will be at Tres Coronas for a while," he said. "Furtado Gomez's place has been padlocked by the Border Patrol officials. It won't open for some time—not until the Treasury Department has confiscated that counterfeiting plant."

They groped back along the dark alley beside the jail and saw a light burning in Stockton's front office. Texanna left Roy's side to run up the porch steps, opening the door without knocking in her eagerness to see Tommy again.

Roy saw the girl run over to where the young

sheriff sat at his desk, reading a letter.

After an interval, he stepped up to the office door, clearing his throat loudly. He heard Sheriff Stockton say, "Someone slipped this letter under my door while I was eating supper tonight, honey. What do you make of it?"

Halted in the doorway, Roy saw Texanna Conroy's face go bone-white as she read the note.

"Why—this is a frame-up!" the girl cried. "Tommy, you can't believe this. It isn't so!"

Stockton came to his feet, shrugging. "Just the same, I can't pass up any leads, Texanna. Any idea where Roy Rogers is?"

"Right here, Tommy," Roy called from the doorway. "What's up?"

Stockton whirled, his face grim as he caught sight of the cowboy framed in the jailhouse door. The sheriff's hand dropped to his gun, but before he could draw it Texanna ran across the office and thrust the sheet of paper into Roy's hand.

Holding it around to the lamplight, Roy read the crudely printed letters.

Sheriff:

Next time you have the chance, look in Texas Ranger Roy Rogers's saddlebags. You'll discover he ain't a ranger, but an outlaw.

A Friend

Roy handed the paper back to Texanna.

"Well," he said, smiling ruefully, "let's have a look in my saddlebags, Tommy. You'll find a first-aid kit and my field glasses and a spare shirt and pair of socks. Anything criminal about that?"

A sheepish look crossed Stockton's face.

"Let's have a look at those saddle pouches, shall we?" he said. "I've already checked with San Antonio, Roy, and Ranger headquarters telegraphed me that they have no one named Roy Rogers on their roster."

Heading out toward the jail alley, Roy said calmly, "Of course not. I told you this badge belonged to John Whetlaw. Ranger headquarters doesn't know I came here with John."

They reached the back of the jail where Trigger and Texanna's horse were silhouetted in the pink glow of the locomotive firebox. Texanna had remained at the jail office.

Grinning tolerantly, Roy Rogers unbuckled the off saddlebag. By the light streaming from a dance hall next door to the jail, Tommy Stockton inspected the bag's contents—field glasses and extra clothing, a package of letters, a box of .45 cartridges.

"Now the other one," Roy said, taunting Stockton for his suspicious nature. "I don't see anything illegal so far."

Roy and the sheriff walked around Trigger and the lawman stood by in embarrassment as Roy unbuckled the other saddlebag.

"Have a good look, friend," Roy said jauntily, stepping aside. "So I'm a desperado in disguise, eh?"

Stockton thrust a hand into the open bag and drew forth a peculiar white object that looked like a sugar sack. Drawn on this cloth sack was the face of a leering skull!

As Rogers stared aghast, Tommy Stockton pawed again into the pouch and lifted out a black shirt with white riblike designs stitched on it. Below the shirt was a pair of black chaps with hip and leg bones inlaid in white leather.

"Why—that's the disguise costume of the Ghost of Mystery Rancho!" Roy exclaimed. "How—how did that come to be planted in—"

Tommy Stockton whirled to face Roy, the lamplight flashing on his sheriff's star. Stuffing the Ghost's costume back into the saddlebag with his left hand, Stockton drew a six-gun from leather with his right, aiming it point-blank at Roy Rogers's belt buckle.

"I'm arresting you, Ghost!" Stockton bit out. "This evidence can't be passed off as a joke. This costume and this mask have put a reign of terror in the Basin too long for me to take chances. I've got to jail you till I've proved you innocent, Roy Rogers!"

CHAPTER XVIII

LYNCH LAW IN GUNSIGHT!

Old Buck Conroy was in the Silver Dollar, relaxing with some of his Gunsight cronies, when he first heard the news that swept the town.

A stranger believed to be the dreaded Ghost of Mystery Rancho had been arrested by Sheriff Stockton, and even now was behind bars.

The old cattleman drew the first easy breath he had enjoyed in months of strain and worry.

"Boys," he said, "this news is too much. I didn't expect to live to see this day. I'll leave you now. I want to have a look at this suspect Tommy corraled."

Leaving the Silver Dollar, Conroy found the town in feverish excitement.

The Ghost's name was on every lip as Conroy hurried up the street—*Roy Rogers!*

Hearing that name, Conroy was both skeptical and outraged. Was it possible that the handsome and likable young waddy who had enjoyed the hospitality of Box C these past few days was the fiend who had slaughtered his cattle, burned his graze, murdered his line riders, blinded his foreman?

Reaching the jail, Conroy had to force his way

through a clamoring throng of excited miners and riffraff gathered there in hopes of getting a glimpse of the captured Ghost.

Inside Stockton's office, the Box C owner found his daughter and Tommy Stockton engaged in a violent argument. This was the first trouble ever to come between these two so far as Buck Conroy knew.

As her father entered, Texanna rushed to him and flung her arms about his shoulders, weeping bitterly.

"Somebody's framed Roy, Dad," the girl choked, "and Tommy here is being a stubborn fool—he's got Roy locked up—"

The young sheriff met Conroy's eyes reluctantly, his cheeks aflame.

"I know it sounds loco, Buck," Stockton confessed, "but somebody—a member of his gang who decided to double-cross him, I guess—tipped me off to look in Roy's saddlebags. I found the costume he uses when riding as the Ghost—"

Conroy heard these details in shocked silence.

Texanna turned on the man she planned to marry, her eyes snapping like sparks.

"It's absurd," she said. "I saw the Ghost today—I shared Roy's experience in being hurled into the Well of Bones, as I've just been telling Tommy. Yet he won't listen to me."

Stockton spread his palms in a helpless gesture.

"I find it hard to believe Roy is guilty," he said

to Buck, "but as sheriff I know my duty."

Texanna cut in angrily. "Any one of a hundred people could have slipped the Ghost's disguise into Roy's saddlebags without being seen, it's so dark behind the jail where the hitchrack is located. Oh, Daddy, why is Tommy so stubborn?"

Pure misery shone in Stockton's eyes, but there was a stubborn set to his jaws.

"It won't hurt Rogers to stay in jail a few days until I have led a raid through that tunnel he told us about and bring in Señor Rattlesnake's gang," Stockton said. "I've wired the Texas Rangers in Austin to send me a company of Rangers to make that raid. If Señor Rattlesnake identifies Roy as the Ghost—"

Texanna seized her father's arm and dragged him to the office door.

"Come on, Pop!" the girl said angrily. "Tommy won't even let me into the bull pen to talk to Roy. Let's get out of here. I don't want to speak to Tommy again till I cool off."

Out in the darkness, Buck Conroy escorted his daughter away from the crowd in front of the jail.

"We'll spend the night at the Trail House, Texie girl," the old rancher said gently. "If I only had some cash, I'd try to go Roy's bail."

Conroy took his daughter to the rambling two-story hotel building and booked adjoining rooms for the night. Texanna went upstairs, leaving her father in the lobby.

The Box C rancher was lighting a cigar, trying to study the thing out to his own satisfaction, when one of his former cowpunchers poked his head in the door and shouted, "Hi, boss! You suffered the most from the Ghost's hands—you won't want to miss the lynchin' bee!"

The cheroot fell from Conroy's lips as he stared at the excited young buckaroo.

"Lynching? What are you talking about, Slim?"

"Why that *mestizo* wrangler of yours, Bronc Alamar—he's over at the Comanche bar, feedin' the boys free likker by the barrel an' whippin' 'em into a frenzy. They aim to bust into the jail tonight an' drag this Rogers hombre out an' string him up, Buck! We don't want to miss the fun!"

In spite of the infirmities of his age, Buck Conroy found himself sprinting up the main street with Slim, toward the false-fronted Comanche Saloon, hangout of the town's tougher element.

Kerosene flares pulsed and guttered along the saloon's front as the Box C boss and his former waddy fought their way into the crowd which was trying to push through the batwings.

It was impossible to get inside the barroom, but through the wide-open windows Buck Conroy could see his cavvy wrangler, Bronc Alamar, standing up on a barrel and haranguing the crowd.

"Yuh know what the Ghost has done to Mystery Rancho," Alamar bellowed, waving a bottle. "Yuh all know what he done to our ramrod, Jingo Bates —blinded him for life with burnin' oil, just because Jingo wouldn't sell out to him."

A roar of voices blotted out the agitator's voice, hoarse calls like those Buck Conroy had heard before, in other Texas cow towns in the Nueces country. Lynch law had come to Gunsight tonight, and once aroused, Conroy knew no power on earth could save Roy Rogers from the violence of a mob.

"What are we goin' to do about this?" Alamar's shrill voice continued. "The Ghost is roostin' over in Tom Stockton's calaboose right this minute, waitin' for his gang from acrost the Rio to hear about his arrest an' come to his resy-cue. The sheriff wants to hold this Rogers hombre fer trial by jury. Did the Ghost o' Mystery Rancho give any chance to the hombres he bushwhacked out in the Basin?"

Ill in heart and spirit, Buck Conroy turned away. He heard the mob's answer to Bronc Alamar, "Lynch the polecat! Gun down Tommy Stockton if'n he interferes. Drag Roy Rogers out by the ears!"

Hardly knowing what he was doing, old Buck returned to the Trail House and knocked on Tex-anna's door. When the girl unlocked the door and faced her father, old Buck said gravely, "Daughter, heck's about to bust loose in town tonight. Bronc's getting a lynch mob drunk enough to storm the jail. I'm afraid Tommy won't be able to hold 'em. And Roy Rogers—"

Texanna stiffened as if she had suffered a physical blow. She brushed a hand across her tear-wet eyes and said desperately, "We've got to do something before the mob marches on the jail, Dad."

"There's nothing we *can* do, Texie. We're out-numbered. The mob will cool off by tomorrow, but that will be too late. I know Tommy will go down fightin' to defend his prisoner, but—"

Texanna snatched her white sombrero off a wall peg and brushed past her father.

"I'll do something!" she flung back over her shoulder, and before Buck Conroy could reach out to interfere, his daughter was racing down the corridor to the lobby stairs.

Leaving the Trail House, Texanna saw a large crowd blocking the main street in front of the Comanche bar. She saw blazing torches and bobbing lanterns, and read in those signs the fact that Bronc Alamar's lynchmen would soon be marching on the jail. Ducking down an alley between a general store and a blacksmith shop, Texanna Conroy raced toward the Gunsight jail.

Reaching the jail, she saw that the crowd had dispersed to join Alamar's lynchers farther down the street. That was an ominous sign. Even Gunsight's level-headed citizens, apparently, had caught the hanging-bee fever.

She found Stockton's door locked and bolted, but the sheriff, grim-faced and wearing two guns, opened it when he recognized his fiancée's frantic calls.

"Tommy, you can't stand off Alamar's mob alone," the girl said frantically. "You've got to get Roy out of town while there's time."

Stockton shook his head grimly and tapped the walnut stock of the double-barreled shotgun cradled across his arms.

"This is a brick jail," he said, "and Alamar's mob can't breach the iron door out back. He's got to come through my office to reach the cell block. Alamar won't get far with a couple charges of Number Four buckshot in his brisket. When that happens, the mob will break up fast enough."

Texanna groaned. "They'll shoot through the door—they'll kill you, Tommy," she said. "Your sense of duty—"

Stockton pointed toward the door, the danger of his position putting its fighting glint in his eyes.

"Get back to the hotel, Texanna. I'll handle this."

Knowing the inflexible bravery of the man she was to wed, the girl knew she had lost. Stockton could not be deterred from making his hopeless stand in this jail.

"They'll Kill You, Tommy," Texanna Cried

"Where's Roy's horse?" she said, stalling for time.

"Still hitched out back. I haven't had time to stable Trigger yet."

Turning to leave, Texanna saw Roy Rogers's six-guns resting on the sheriff's desk. Before Stockton could intervene, she snatched up the heavy Peace-maker .45's and fled out the door, Stockton's startled yell following her.

Glancing down the street, Texanna saw the black tide of Alamar's small army of blood-hungry killers moving up the main street toward the jail. They were only a block away. Minutes counted now.

She headed along the alley that ran along the jail wall, her only plan being to call Roy Rogers to the window of his cell and pass the bayed cowboy pris-oner his guns. At least he could die defending his life from the mob.

As Texanna reached the rear of the jail, she saw the fireman of the mining company's railroad engine oiling the drive-rods of the locomotive.

In that moment, an idea was born in Texanna's brain.

Rounding the hitchrack where Roy's palomino and her line-back dun stood, she approached the railroad man with jutting six-guns.

Recognizing the oiler, the girl cried out, "Clem, you've got a lot of chain in the tender of your engine, haven't you? I've seen it when you and the engineer took me for joy-rides in the cab."

Clem eyed the leveled guns. His face went ashen in the light of the lantern he held.

"Yeah, the chains are there, ma'am," Clem stammered. "But go easy with them smokepoles, girl."

Texanna came closer to the fireman.

"Clem, listen to me. A drunken mob is heading for the jail to kill Tommy Stockton and hang an innocent man in one of those cells. I want you to hook a chain on your cowcatcher and fasten it to the bars of that prisoner's cell. I want you to yank those bars out by the roots with this locomotive!"

The locomotive fireman backed away from the menace of Texanna's leveled guns.

"But—but helpin' a prisoner escape—I'd be throwed in jail—"

Texanna's thumbs eased the gun hammers back to full cock.

"Would you rather have me shoot you, Clem?" she said icily. "I'm in earnest about this thing. You've got to hurry."

Already the wolf-pack roar of Bronc Alamar's advancing lynchmen was a heavy, dull booming in the night.

Cringing from the guns in Texanna's hands, Clem climbed into the cab of his engine and came out with a heavy length of logging chain. He was barely able to stagger under its bulk. Great iron hooks were on either end of the chain which was used for moving ore cars at the shaft houses.

Texanna's shout brought Roy Rogers's face to one of the barred windows in the back of the jail, his features white in the glare of the locomotive headlight which was pointed at the wall of the building.

While Texanna explained the situation to Roy, Clem attached the heavy chain securely to the coupling bar of the engine's cowcatcher, which faced the sidetrack bumper barely five feet from the base of the jail wall.

Then, grunting with the effort of lifting the heavy chain, Clem handed the other hook up to where Roy could clutch it, the railroader standing on the earthen bumper of the track.

From the front of the jail came Bronc Alamar's booming voice as the lynch mob halted on the street. "Sheriff, we're comin' in to get the Ghost and hang him. Don't stop us."

Metal clanged as Roy Rogers laced the chain through the heavy iron bars of the cell window and fastened the hook.

As Clem hurried back to the locomotive cab, Texanna heard Tommy Stockton's defiant yell from inside the jail office.

"The first man who tries to bash open that door gets a double charge of buckshot, Alamar!"

CHAPTER XIX

ON THE DODGE

Clem reversed his gear lever and reached for the throttle bar on the boiler head of the locomotive.

From his position in the engine cab, the fireman could see up the alley to where Alamar's lynch mob was waiting, knowing that sure death from flying buckshot would greet the first man to attempt storming the jailhouse.

Feeding live steam to the cylinders, Clem started the engine backing down the sidetrack. The big chain picked up its loops, straightened out.

The big drivewheels revolved. Sparks and smoke erupted from the engine's funnel-shaped stack.

And then, as simply as jerking a picket pin out of wet earth, the iron casing and latticed bars of Roy Rogers's jail cell were yanked out of the brick wall.

Roy Rogers swung his legs through the opening as Clem closed his throttle and braked the engine to a stop. Leaning from the handrails of the engine cab, Clem saw Roy jump down to the weed-grown bumper where the rails ended. He saw Texanna hand the escaping prisoner her guns, saw Roy yell his brief thanks to the girl and then sprint toward the horses at the hitchrack.

Roy Rogers vaulted into Trigger's saddle and wheeled the magnificent palomino away from the rack.

"Good luck, Roy!" Texanna shouted into the night, and then the fugitive was spurring at a full gallop past Clem's railway engine, flashing the scared fireman a grin of gratitude as he passed the cab.

Clem, knowing the consequences of what he had done, leaped down the cab steps and raced off into the darkness.

Texanna, hearing the swift beat of Trigger's hoofs dying down-canyon as Roy Rogers fled from Gunsight and the mob's wrath, filled her lungs with a glad breath of thanksgiving.

Then, remembering the danger Sheriff Tommy Stockton faced, Texanna ran up the alley and climbed the saloon porch.

Bronc Alamar was arguing with a group of men who were holding a wagon tongue they planned to use as a battering ram to smash down Stockton's door.

The girl's auburn tresses gleamed in the torchlight as Texanna addressed the lynch mob, "You're too late, men. Roy Rogers has escaped. He tore out the bars of his cell window and escaped!"

Instantly Bronc Alamar and his hanging mob forgot about Sheriff Stockton, waiting with his shotgun inside the darkened jail office.

"Come on, men!" Alamar shouted. "We'll see if the gal is lyin'. If she is, I'll cut her throat!"

The mob jostled its way into the alley, dividing into two groups as they rounded the brick jail. A moment later their angry shouts were proof that they had discovered the open window of Roy's cell.

Tommy Stockton opened the door and peered out at Texanna.

"You helped Roy get away?" he asked grimly.

The girl nodded. "He's not the Ghost, Tommy, and you know it."

Stockton brushed past her, heading down the alley to where waited the hundred-odd men who a moment before had been seeking his life.

Glancing at the broken casing of Roy's cell, Stockton shouted to Alamar's mob, "Men, I'm posting a thousand-dollar reward for Roy Rogers's capture, dead or alive. Get your horses. I have a hunch I know where Rogers will head. The Rio Grande—and Mexico—"

Ten minutes later, Roy Rogers reined up Trigger to give his mount a chance to blow.

He was on a high ridge overlooking the cross-hatched pattern of lights marking Gunsight town.

Sitting his saddle there, the fugitive rider caught sight of a flood of riders storming out of Gunsight, lamplight flashing on rifle barrels as they swept through the outskirts of town.

Roy groaned, knowing who those riders were. Sheriff Stockton was leading a posse after him. Roy knew he was on the dodge now, a hunted man, perhaps an outlaw with a bounty on his scalp. He had little doubt but that Stockton had issued shoot-on-sight orders.

"Come on, Trigger," Roy said to the palomino, wheeling his horse around. "I'm depending on you to out-strip that posse of Stockton's."

Reaching the flats of Tomahawk Basin, Roy Rogers was not sure where to go next. He could not fort up at Box C; to do that would be to invite suicide. He thought of the line-camp cabin in Skeleton Canyon, but vetoed that refuge.

There was Haunted Mission; he would be safe beyond the tunnel which led to the Well of Bones, and quite possibly the Ghost of Mystery Rancho might show up there.

Then he thought of Señor Rattlesnake's den, and for reasons he was not completely sure of, Roy Rogers headed Trigger toward the Rio Grande.

Across the night he heard the thunder of hoofs in the wind, and suddenly realized that Tommy Stockton might head directly to the quicksand *sumidero*, knowing as he did of the existence of Señor Rattlesnake's secret cave under the Rio Grande.

To shake off his pursuit, Roy turned Trigger back

toward the Navajada foothills, and headed into a canyon which he believed would take him to high ground where he could cut in behind the Gunsight posse and watch their movements.

Twenty minutes later disaster faced him in the form of a high blank wall of granite, hundreds of feet from canyon bottom to rimrock. Not knowing this country, Roy had blundered into a box gorge!

When daylight came, Stockton's posse would track him here. He would have to get out into the Basin without delay.

But Roy had not figured on the speed the Gunsight posse would make.

As he put Trigger out of the box canyon's mouth, a sudden roar of gunshots greeted him from the higher slope to the north.

Wheeling the palomino around, Roy saw an appalling sight. Stockton and his posse riders had discovered him! Through the moonlight, Rogers could see the Gunsight sheriff and his men racing at breakneck speed down the mountain slope, the red flashes of their guns proof enough that he was their target.

So far, he was out of range of any gun less than a .45-70. Shooting from horseback, it was doubtful if his pursuers could cut Trigger down at this distance.

Again Rogers headed toward the Rio Grande and the means of crossing into Mexico which Señor Rattlesnake's tunnel offered. The smuggler country on the Chihuahua bank could hardly be any more dangerous than the soil of Texas tonight, with that wolf pack of armed killers pounding on his trail.

Tonight, more than ever before, Roy Rogers was thankful for Trigger's speed and stamina.

Rogers was out of sight of the pursuing riders and a good mile and a quarter in front of them when the lather-flecked palomino brought him at last to the foot of the butte where the quicksand bog barred further progress toward the Rio.

Sheering away from the deadly sands, Rogers put Trigger down into the brush-choked draw where he had left his horse on the other occasion when the ill-fated Fung Ling had retrieved the palomino for him.

Deep in the tangled chaparral between the draw's eroded rock walls, Rogers dismounted and stripped Trigger of saddle and bridle. He could not take the time to reach the cavern door and trundle the plank gangway across the *sumidero* so that Trigger could accompany him to Mexico.

"Stockton may discover you here, Trigger, but Texanna will see that you're well taken care of till we meet again," Roger told the jaded palomino. "Let's hope that won't be too long."

In the act of caching his silver-mounted saddle in the brush, Roy thought of something.

He saw that his saddlebags were still open. Reaching in the nigh pouch, a laugh escaped his lips.

So rapidly had events moved in Gunsight tonight, the sheriff had not had time to carry the Ghost's costume into his office!

With hands that trembled with eagerness, Roy Rogers shook out the skull mask and fitted it over his head, completely concealing his features. Adjusting the slits in the skull mask in front of his eyes, Roy then donned the Ghost's vest with its riblike pattern and pulled on the black leather chaps with their hip and leg bone design.

Thus disguised as the most-wanted outlaw in Texas, the mysterious fiend who had made Mystery Rancho a range to be shunned by cowboys, Roy Rogers scrambled up out of the draw.

Off to the northeast he saw Tommy Stockton's posse approaching as fast as they could urge their exhausted horses.

A laugh came from behind the Ghost's mask as Roy Rogers scaled the shoulder of the butte.

Minutes later, as Stockton's posse came within gunshot of where he stood, Roy Rogers caught sight of the rope he had left dangling from the knob of rock on the occasion of his first visit to this place, less than a week ago.

His skeleton-costumed figure was an invisible blur against the granite face of the butte as he slid down the rope into the chaparral which hid the door of Señor Rattlesnake's cavern.

He was groping his way toward that door when he heard the rusty hinges squeak and out into the brush stepped the sinister, serape-draped figure of Mexico's king of smugglers, Señor Rattlesnake himself.

The smuggler was leading a horse, and he carried a lighted candle. Its feeble rays revealed the skull mask and skeleton costume of the man standing at arm's length away.

"Señor Ghost!" exclaimed the Mexican outlaw, hastily blowing out his candle. "What brings you here tonight, *amigo?*"

Roy Rogers lifted a finger to the mouth of his mask and spoke in gutteral Spanish, imitating the Ghost's hoarse voice.

"Ran into trouble at Gunsight tonight, Señor Rattlesnake. Those riders out beyond the *sumidero*—they are Sheriff Stockton and his men who chased me to this spot."

Señor Rattlesnake grunted in the darkness, as they stood side by side peering out through the brush. Stockton and his riders had reined up on the solid ground beyond the quicksand, obeying the young sheriff's warning to avoid the *sumidero*.

"You led them to our secret?" Señor Rattlesnake asked in an aggrieved voice.

"It was either that or die before Señor Stockton's guns," Roy Rogers retorted. "Hush—listen—"

Sheriff Stockton was addressing his riffraff posse-men.

"Bronc, Yates, all of you—listen to me. The Ghost has made good his escape. He's got a tunnel leading under the Rio at this point. I will not attempt to lead you into an ambush across the river tonight. That's a job for the Texas Rangers."

Bronc Alamar's voice came wearily through the night to the ears of Señor Rattlesnake and the disguised Roy Rogers.

"A *bueno* idea, Sheriff. This is too dangerous a spot to hang around. We go back to town, no?"

Roy Rogers saw the sheriff nod as he picked up his reins.

"We had tough luck tonight," he said, "letting the Ghost slip through our fingers. No hard feelings, boys. I can understand why you wanted to lynch that villain."

As the disgruntled posse turned their horses and headed back over the ridge out of sight, Roy Rogers turned to Señor Rattlesnake and said huskily in Spanish,

"*Amigo,* we must leave your hide-out forever. To-night, before the sheriff brings the Texas *Rangeros* to raid us. For the time being, we must hide out in the Lone Star State—at the Well of Bones. It is our only chance to escape capture."

CHAPTER XX

UNDER-RIVER EXPLOSIVES

In the darkness, Roy Rogers heard the Mexican smuggler emit a deep groan.

"All our plans to seize Mystery Rancho—we must give them up, Señor Ghost?"

Roy shrugged. "What else can we do, *amigo?*"

Señor Rattlesnake rubbed his pock-marked jaw for a moment.

"The Texas *Rangeros* have no authority out of Texas," the smuggler pointed out jubilantly. "We can sit tight, as the gringos say, and wait until this thing blows over."

Roy had anticipated that argument and had his answer ready promptly. "No, Señor Rattlesnake. This is an international business, breaking up our partnership. The Rangers will bring the Mexican *rurale* police into this deal. For all we know, they may have telegraphed the *rurales* down at the provincial capital in Chihuahua City by now. Who knows? There may be a company of *rurale* policemen heading north to the Rio Grande tonight as we stand here wasting time."

Roy could almost see the smuggler chief shrivel

up as he thought over this dismaying news.

"Esta bueno," Señor Rattlesnake said finally. "Come. We will get back to my *casa* without delay."

The two men headed into the tunnel mouth and the Mexican closed the door behind them. Then he relighted his stub of tallow candle, and they made their way under the Rio Grande and out the doorway at the foot of the Chihuahua trail.

On their way into the canyon, Roy Rogers said casually, "How many of the band are here now, Señor?"

Señor Rattlesnake gave the impostor at his side a peculiar look, making Rogers wonder if he had said the wrong thing.

"Your memory is short, Señor Ghost." The smuggler king laughed. "Panchito and Camarillo have gone to San Carlos to pick up the golden candlesticks from the church there. You say you can sell them for a profit."

Roy's cheeks ballooned with relief under the skull mask. He realized he was playing a desperate game here, masquerading as the Ghost of Mystery Rancho. A single wrong word, the slightest misstep, might arouse the suspicions of this deadly outlaw.

His voice was the thing that would give him away quickest, for he was the same general build as the real Ghost and the skeleton costume fit him perfectly. But he knew that safety lay in talking little.

"Oh, yes," Roy said. "I had forgotten about the San Carlos deal. The—others in the band are here?"

This time, Señor Rattlesnake came to a dead stop.

"Have you gone loco?" demanded the smuggler. "It was at your suggestion, Señor Ghost, that I let them take a holiday at El Corazon. You said we would carry on no more smuggling until you were sure Roy Rogers was dead."

Roy kept still, knowing how close was the line between life and death for him now. Having heard of Señor Rattlesnake's blinding speed on the draw, he did not want to blunder into a shoot-out here.

Señor Rattlesnake laughed then, and clapped Roy on the shoulder as they resumed their trek along the narrow canyon ledge.

"As soon as I knew you had thrown this Señor Rogers into the Well of Bones," he said, "I sent Cabral Mendazoa to El Corazon to bring our men back, ready for duty. They will arrive some time tonight. In time, I am sure, to reach the safety of Haunted Mission before the Rangers attack us."

When they reached the hut where Roy had spied on Señor Rattlesnake's meeting with the smugglers from China a few nights ago, the smuggler king went inside and lighted the wick of a pottery bowl lamp filled with oil.

Señor Rattlesnake had recovered his composure now, but there was bitter defeat in his eyes as he

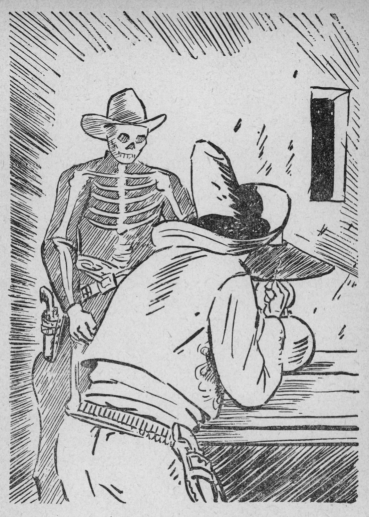

Señor Rattlesnake Lit the Lamp

stared around at the cabin.

"It grieves me to think of giving this up," he said. "It hurts to think that the young gringo, Roy Rogers, was the one who let the *Americanos* know of our tunnel, and of this place."

Roy Rogers sat down on a bench and laughed villainously.

"I imagine Señor Rogers will still be alive when we reach the Well of Bones," he said. "You can have the pleasure of torturing him if you wish, *amigo*."

Señor Rattlesnake unlocked a wall cupboard and drew out a bottle of Mexican brandy.

"It is too bad you cannot drink with me because of your *calavera* mask, Señor," the outlaw said, pouring himself a drink of the fiery liquor. "We have been *compadres* a long time now, *amigo*, ever since you found the ancient Spanish chart in the Haunted Mission which disclosed the location of our tunnel under the Rio Grande, and looked me up over in San Castro to form our partnership in the contraband business."

Roy's heart thumped with excitement. It was the Ghost, then, who had stumbled on the secret of the underground passage linking Texas with Mexico; Señor Rattlesnake must have shifted the scene of his smuggling activity to this spot after joining in partnership with the Ghost of Mystery Rancho.

"Yes, *amigo*," Roy said, knowing some reply was

expected from him. "It was a lucky day for us when I discovered that Spanish map. I am as sorry as you that we have to move on to other fields."

Señor Rattlesnake, gulping from a long draught of the brandy, arched his brows in surprise.

"You will leave Box C, Señor?"

Roy shrugged.

"Why should I stay, Señor Rattlesnake? Now that the secret of our tunnel is known to the Texas Rangers? We cannot use it for smuggling again."

Señor Rattlesnake's frown worried Roy. He knew he was skating on extremely thin ice.

"But Mystery Rancho is a money-maker. You will have to give up being the Ghost, of course. Then Box C will return to normal. Is it not so?"

Roy pretended to think this over. What was Señor Rattlesnake driving at? Did he believe that the Ghost was Buck Conroy? Roy had been under the impression that the Ghost's identity was known to no one, not even Señor Rattlesnake—yet obviously that was not true.

"Since you insist on keeping your mask on, even in front of me," Señor Rattlesnake laughed, scratching his rattlesnake-tattooed arm, "you will no doubt want to sleep. Your regular bed is prepared as usual. For myself, I will keep watch, in case the *rurale* police should come this night."

Roy felt his heart sink. His regular bed was prepared as usual—but how did he know where that bed was located?

He stood up, stretching and yawning.

"Bed will feel good," he said, "but before I sleep tonight, there is a little errand I must run, across the Rio. I—er—dropped something in my haste to escape the sheriff's posse."

Heading toward the door, knowing that this remark had not seemed false to his host, Roy Rogers said, "When can we expect Mendoza back with the men?"

Señor Rattlesnake consulted a big gold watch.

"I'm afraid not before daylight, *amigo*. If we hear signs of the Rangers coming through our tunnel, we can of course escape on the north trail, you and I."

Anxious to get out of this situation—every bit of conversation he indulged in at this point was packed with danger to his masquerade—Roy Rogers left the cabin and headed down the narrow canyon trail.

Crossing the tunnel under the Rio Grande, Roy decided against trundling the gangplank out across the quicksand bog, and instead climbed his rope to the top of the bluff.

The pink stain of approaching dawn was glowing behind the Navajada peaks now, but the coming of daylight occasioned him no particular worry.

He knew that Stockton would not return to this spot with a Ranger troop for at least a week; before that time Roy hoped to have trapped the entire Señor Rattlesnake smuggling band.

Climbing down the west shoulder of the butte, Roy headed for the draw where he had left Trigger. But it was not the palomino Roy was after, this morning. He had an entirely different scheme in mind.

A few minutes later he was burrowing in the brush for the gunny sack full of dynamite and percussion caps which he had brought here from Skeleton Canyon, the explosives which Bronc Alamar had planted under his bed at the line-camp cabin.

Picking up the gunny sack load of dynamite, Roy returned to the top of the bluff, slid down the rope and again entered the old Spanish tunnel under the river.

When he had reached the level stretch of tunnel which he knew to be under the river bed, Roy lighted a stub of candle he had brought from Señor Rattlesnake's *casa* and sized up the most likely spot to plant the dynamite.

He had no fuse, but that was not important. Very carefully, Roy Rogers rolled back the opening of the gunny sack and stuck the candle to the burlap fabric with hot wax. Then he took what paper he had on his person, crumpled it up, and wadded it into the sack alongside the sticks of dynamite, in such a position that the candle flame would ignite the paper.

Snuffing out the candle, Roy Rogers headed on down the tunnel, counting his paces so as to locate quickly the hidden explosives on his return trip.

The ceiling of the cavern was not thick; he could hear the movement of the Rio Grande's waters through the rock. The dynamite, when set off by fire, would undoubtedly cause a portion of the rock ceiling to give way, allowing the Rio Grande to come pouring into the ancient Spanish cavern.

When he got back to Señor Rattlesnake's *casa* he found the smuggler posted outside with a high-power rifle across his knees. The outlaw was watching both directions of the canyon, fearful of Rangers coming from the north and Mexican *rurale* police from the south.

"As long as you're doing lookout duty, *amigo*," Roy Rogers said drowsily, "I'll get some sleep. Awake me if necessary." He paused. "I think," he said, "I'll sleep in the barn, Señor Rattlesnake. I'd like to be close to the horses in case of surprise attack."

Señor Rattlesnake grinned venomously.

"I have two *caballos* saddled and ready," he said.

Going to the barn where the other night he had knocked out the Mexican smuggler, Pedro, Roy pulled down enough hay in a stall to make a bed.

Then he stretched out and was almost instantly asleep.

CHAPTER XXI

SMUGGLERS' ESCAPE

The day ran its course and blue twilight was pooling between the rimrocks of the outlaws' lair when Roy Rogers was awakened by Señor Rattlesnake.

Crowding the small barn behind the smuggler king were eight other Mexicans, all wearing expressions of extreme nervousness. All were fatigued from a long hard ride through this day's heat from San Castro town.

"I saw no sign of *rurales* or Texas *Rangeros,* amigo," Señor Rattlesnake said, "so I let you sleep. Mendoza and our *compadres* only now returned here."

Roy glared at the cowering smugglers through the eye-holes in his skull mask.

"Why so long a delay, coming from San Castro?" he demanded with well-feigned anger.

One of the Mexicans—Roy guessed he was Mendoza, the messenger—stepped forward.

"I found our *compañeros* dead drunk, Señor Ghost," the courier explained. "I had to wait until they were sober enough to ride, it is so."

Roy dismissed the shivering smugglers with a

shrug of his shoulders.

"Very well," he said, turning to Señor Rattlesnake. "It is best that we have the cover of night for crossing the Basin to reach Haunted Mission. Are we ready to start?"

Señor Rattlesnake looked startled.

"You have not eaten, Señor," the smuggler chief reminded the fake Ghost of Mystery Rancho. "There is no food at Haunted Mission except what we take with us. Surely you think we have time for you to eat and drink?"

Rogers laughed harshly, wondering how the real Ghost would sound if he ever gave vent to mirth.

"*Seguramente,*" he chuckled. "I am very hungry."

Reaching the cabin, Roy found a hot meal of *enchiladas, frijoles,* tortillas and delicious *tacos* spread out on the table.

While he was eating—apparently the others in Señor Rattlesnake's band were too frightened to have any appetite—the smuggler chieftain explained that he had loaded three pack mules with food supplies to last them while they were hiding out at Haunted Mission, two more mules bearing *ollas* of fresh water, and another six mules whose packs contained contraband—drugs, stolen gold, and other items of plunder kept stored here—which he saw no use in leaving for the *rurales* to find.

It was pitch dark when Roy Rogers left the cabin,

his stomach filled with well-cooked Mexican food.

He found the eight smugglers waiting impatiently with their horses. When Señor Rattlesnake led two saddle broncs out of the barn, one for Roy's use, the fake Ghost shook his head.

"I have a palomino stashed out in a *barranca* on the Texan side of the river," he said. "Roy Rogers's pony. I decided to use his palomino from now on."

Señor Rattlesnake laughed.

"Roy Rogers will not need a *caballo,*" the outlaw jeered, "down in the Well of Bones, no?"

A few minutes later the cavalcade of riders and the string of pack mules were heading down the twisting ledge trail, with the skeleton-costumed Roy Rogers walking in the lead alongside Señor Rattlesnake's stirrup.

Entering the tunnel, however, Roy Rogers dropped behind, saying he would keep the pack animals moving.

Strung out in single file, Señor Rattlesnake and his smuggler band headed through the sooty blackness of the underground passage.

Roy Rogers, carefully counting his paces, halted when he neared the location of his dynamite cache.

He groped with his hands along the dripping walls until he found the cavity where the sack of dynamite was concealed.

Then, drawing a match from his sombrero band, he lighted the stub of candle.

It took a moment or two to arrange the scrap paper in such a way that this inflammable material would not light until the candle had burned a half inch down. By that time, he knew he would be safely out of the Spanish cavern.

Racing on after the smuggler train, Roy caught up with the end of the pack mule string just as Señor Rattlesnake was running the plank gangway out across the quicksand bog.

There was a slight delay while Señor Rattlesnake scouted the Texas landscape, fearful lest Sheriff Stockton had posted guards at this end of the tunnel.

Then, satisfied that the coast was clear, the smuggler chief led his henchmen across the plank walkway to the safety of solid ground.

The fake Ghost of Mystery Rancho was the last to cross. He said to Señor Rattlesnake, "No need to hide our gangplank now. Let the Rangers go into our tunnel. They will find an empty *casa* across the river, no?"

Bidding the smugglers wait, Roy hurried over to the near-by draw and returned on Trigger.

" '*Sta muy bien*," Rogers said, reining over alongside Señor Rattlesnake at the head of the column. "We will take a beeline across the Basin. Before dawn we will be safe at Haunted Mission."

The procession had barely gotten under way when a terrific underground explosion, from somewhere behind them, blasted the night's stillness. The blast seem to split the earth to its very core, sending echoes bouncing off across the rocky Navajada ridges.

Twisting in saddle, Roy watched for a billow of smoke to issue from the mouth of the dynamited cavern at the Rio's edge. Then he realized that the inrushing waters of the mighty river had swallowed up the smoke of the blast.

"That sounded as though it came from the canyon," Mendoza exclaimed. "The *rurales* must be firing on our cabin with cannon, no?"

"It was not thunder," Señor Rattlesnake muttered. "Come, let us hurry away from this place. I do not like the sound of it. If the *rurales* are using shrapnel to destroy my *casa*—"

Roy had to give Trigger his head to keep up with the wild flight of Señor Rattlesnake and his henchmen. When the horses were finally exhausted, five miles out across the sage flats of Tomahawk Basin, it was discovered that the heavily laden pack string had been abandoned by Mendoza.

The fugitives held a hasty council of war. Señor Rattlesnake was in favor of abandoning the mules, fearful that they might run into following *rurale* police if they rode back to recover the animals.

Roy Rogers, however, welcomed this delay. It

was urgent that he make a little side trip over to Box C tonight, and this interruption provided an ideal excuse for him.

"What would we use for food at the Well of Bones?" he pointed out. "No, *señores*. We must send two riders back to get the mules, wherever they have stampeded. We may have to roost at Haunted Mission for ten days or more, and we have no water or food there."

Señor Rattlesnake's terrorized followers would have rather challenged the devil himself than to have headed back to the Rio Grande after the missing mules, but two of their number obeyed Señor Rattlesnake's orders without question.

When the two riders had left, Roy Rogers turned to the smuggler chief and said, "You proceed to Haunted Mission. I'm going to have a little scout over in the direction of Box C, just to make sure no riders are out tonight."

Señor Rattlesnake waggled his head dubiously.

"Let it be so," the smuggler said finally. "*Adios,* then. I will meet you at Haunted Mission before sunrise, no?"

The fake Ghost of Mystery Rancho nodded.

"*Hasta la vista.* Take all the horses through the tunnel to the Well of Bones, if you get there before I do."

Wheeling Trigger around, Roy spurred into a

"I Will Meet You at the Haunted Mission."

gallop and vanished in the darkness. Later, reining up, he heard the faint drumming of hoofs as Señor Rattlesnake led his men north toward High Gate and their rendezvous at Haunted Mission.

Roy's destination across the starlit prairie was the Box C, shuttering lights marking the windows of the main house and the bunkshack. He saw a lantern moving around Bronc Alamar's cavvy corral, where a roustabout was attending to his chores.

Approaching Box C from the north, Roy left Trigger in a clump of dwarf piñons near the corner of Buck Conroy's yard. There he removed the stifling skull mask and the Ghost's vest and chaps, stowing them carefully in his saddlebag.

Climbing the fence, Roy moved cautiously across the yard, avoiding the fanwise spread of lights from various windows.

He was heading for the back wing of the house, to the window marking Texanna's room. He had an urgent message to leave here tonight, and Texanna was the only person he could trust.

As he approached Texanna's window with Indian-like stealth, Roy Rogers did not know that he was being watched from a dark window of the ell opposite the girl's room.

Those eyes gave Roy their full and close attention as the cowboy halted under Texanna's window and drummed his fingers on the glass pane.

Roy heard footsteps approach the window. He ducked back as the blind was run up, and Texanna unlocked the sash and leaned out.

"Roy!" Texanna whispered anxiously. "You shouldn't come here! Tommy's got a posse looking for you!"

Being careful to keep out of the window light, Roy said swiftly, "Listen, Texanna. I've got Señor Rattlesnake and his smuggler gang on their way to Haunted Mission tonight. No time to explain details, but I'm posing as the Ghost of Mystery Rancho —thanks to that costume somebody planted in my saddlebags."

Texanna gasped, stunned by Roy's startling news.

"I plan to get the smugglers herded through that tunnel to the Well of Bones," Roy hurried on, "and hold them there until the sheriff can bring a posse to corral them. By the way, is Bronc Alamar out at the bunkhouse tonight?"

"No," Texanna said, "Bronc's with Tommy's posse. They gave Box C a fine-tooth combing this afternoon, before Dad and I got back from town— thinking you might be hiding somewhere on the ranch. Right now, the posse is camped—"

Roy cut in, "No time to waste talking, Texanna. I want you to ride to Gunsight tonight and tell the sheriff what I've just told you. Tell him to bring at least ten men along. Tell him he'll be able to capture every one of the gang except the Ghost himself. And don't you come along to Haunted Mission with the posse, whatever you do—because there's sure to be lots of lead flying when the showdown comes."

Texanna turned away from her window a moment to blow out the lamp.

"Roy," she whispered, "it won't be necessary for me to ride to town after a posse. Tommy and his men are camped down on Lizard Creek, where the bridge is—not a mile from here."

"The posse's camped at the bridge, eh?" Roy said. "Well, then, you just go to bed, Texanna. I'll ride over there and give Tommy Stockton the news myself."

Texanna called out tensely, "No, Roy—you might get shot riding in! Tommy's posted a reward for your capture. And Bronc Alamar's one of his men. You can't—"

Roy came back to the window and whispered to the girl leaning over the sill, "The sheriff will listen to me, Texanna. And by the way—I think I know— I'm almost positive I know—who the Ghost of Mystery Rancho is. I did a lot of thinking about who planted that costume in my saddlebags, when I was sitting in Gunsight's jail. I think the answer will surprise you. This time tomorrow, with luck, you'll know. *Hasta la vista.*"

With that Roy Rogers vanished in the darkness.

CHAPTER XXII

AT HAUNTED MISSION

Leaving Box C on the Gunsight road, Roy Rogers saw the pink gleam of the sheriff's campfire blooming in the night, down among the willows which bordered Lizard Creek.

He realized he was running some risk in approaching the armed camp of the posse that was hunting for him; but he had enough faith in Tommy Stockton's good sense to run that risk.

With the help of the sheriff's men, Rogers felt certain Señor Rattlesnake's band could be overcome, perhaps without the firing of a shot if they worked the showdown right.

Nearing Lizard Creek, Roy pulled Trigger to a walk. From this distance he saw that most of the possemen were hunkered around the fire, their horses picketed on a bench above the willows.

On the chance that Stockton might have nighthawks posted around the camp, Roy reined off the Gunsight road and dismounted behind a cottonwood some fifty yards from the campfire.

Then he called into the night. "Halloo the camp! The sheriff around?"

Roy's shout brought men springing to their feet. A moment later Tommy Stockton's voice answered him.

"I'm the sheriff. Who is it?"

Keeping behind the trunk of the cottonwood, Roy answered, "This is Roy Rogers, Sheriff."

If the cowboy had hurled a hornet's nest into the possemen's midst, the reaction to his words could not have caused more confusion.

Someone hurled a blanket over the campfire to blot out the light which silhouetted the men; Roy heard the thud of spurred boots as possemen jumped for cover, thinking they were marked for ambush attack.

"If this is a joke, feller," Tommy Stockton yelled above the confusion, "you're takin' an awful risk. My men got orders to shoot Rogers on sight and ask questions afterward."

Roy smiled grimly to himself. "I know that, Tommy," he yelled back. "Tell your bloodhounds to hold their fire. I'm coming in for a powwow with you."

Through the darkness, Roy heard scuffling sounds as the possemen scattered, fearful of a trap. Sheriff Stockton rasped a low-voiced order to one of his men, who jerked the smoldering blanket off the campfire.

"My men won't fire on you, Roy," the sheriff yelled, "but we're taking no chances, in case you've got your gang with you. Head straight for the fire, with your hands up. At the first false move from your men, you'll be shot down."

Roy unbuckled his gun belts and looped them over Trigger's saddle horn.

"I'm alone, Tommy," Roy called back, and stepped out into the feeble glow of the campfire. "Alone and unarmed."

Rogers's flesh crawled as he headed slowly toward the camp, knowing some trigger-jittery posseman might get excited and cut down on him.

Sheriff Stockton advanced to meet Roy Rogers, holding a Winchester at waist level.

"No shooting, men!" Stockton warned his posse, who were scattered along the creek bank, covering Rogers's approach. "If Roy's got the nerve to walk into our camp, I don't want any double-cross deal."

A moment later Roy Rogers halted, arms held high, the shuttering campfire revealing that he was not wearing his Colt harness. Sheriff Stockton circled him twice, covering him with his rifle.

"Before you call your men up," Roy said in a low voice, "I want to talk to you, Tommy."

Stockton halted at arm's length, his face strained and deep-lined with fatigue.

"Talk about what?" Stockton demanded suspiciously.

"Do you still think I'm the Ghost?" Roy asked.

The young sheriff hesitated. "Frankly, I'm not

sure. You could have been framed, as Texanna pointed out. But a man in my position can't take chances, Roy."

The possemen were beginning to get up off the ground and head toward their leader. Without taking his eyes off his prisoner, the sheriff shouted a command. "Keep back, men. I want to hear what this man has to tell me."

Speaking in a whisper, Roy Rogers told Tommy Stockton what he had related to Texanna a few minutes before, over at Box C.

"If you take me at my word, Sheriff," Roy concluded earnestly, "we can corral the whole outfit at the Well of Bones. I'm leaving the decision up to your good judgment."

Stockton grounded the stock of his Winchester.

"The fact that you voluntarily gave yourself up tonight," the sheriff mused, "makes me almost convinced of your innocence, Roy. I like you. I don't want to think you're the Ghost."

Roy lowered his arms which were beginning to ache.

"You'll have to trust me the whole way, Tommy," Roy Rogers said. "I've got to ride over to Haunted Mission and set my trap. Your posse will have to show up later, say around eight o'clock tomorrow morning. If you went over to the mission with me, Señor Rattlesnake and the others would high-tail it."

Tommy Stockton was silent for a long while. Finally he reached out a hand to clasp Roy's.

"Texanna has complete faith in you, Rogers," Stockton said. "I respect her judgment. If you're leading me and my men to an ambush trap at the mission—but I'll make this gamble."

The campfire was blazing now, and the waiting possemen saw Sheriff Stockton turn his back to Roy Rogers.

"Gather 'round, men!" the sheriff called. "I want to tell you something."

The posse riders approached, all of them carrying guns in the open, staring at Roy Rogers as if he were a wild beast. Scanning the whiskery faces of the Gunsight lynchmen, Roy caught sight of Bronc Alamar in the background.

Speaking rapidly, Stockton explained the situation, stating that the posse would turn Roy Rogers free to complete his man-trap at Haunted Mission, then ride over to the ruined chapel at eight o'clock in the morning.

When he had finished speaking, a mumble of dissent and approval went through the group. Clearly these men were not as ready to trust Roy Rogers as the sheriff had been.

"The Ghost could have all his gang planted up there to mow us down, Sheriff," spoke up a Gunsight miner. "I'd say string Roy up, here an' now."

During the discussion which followed, one member of the group slipped away through the shadows. It was the sound of fast-running hoofs leaving the possemen's horse cavvy that put an end to the discussion.

"One of our men has coyoted on us," the sheriff said angrily. "Who was it?"

Roy Rogers, playing a hunch, cried out sharply, "Bronc Alamar—speak up!"

There was complete silence in answer to Roy's call.

"That was Bronc who rabbitted on us, Sheriff," a surly voice spoke up.

Roy Rogers seized Stockton's arm.

"I don't like this, Tommy," he said. "Alamar may try to tip off Señor Rattlesnake about our plans. I'd better ride."

The posse was solidly behind him now, Roy sensed. Tommy Stockton slapped the cowboy on the back.

"Hit the breeze, son," the sheriff said. "I'll hold up and follow you in a couple of hours. We'll show up at the mission at eight o'clock sharp."

Roy Rogers elbowed his way out of the group and broke into a run, back to the cottonwood where Trigger waited.

He buckled on his gun belts, vaulted into saddle, and set the palomino off across the sagebrush flats at a gallop, heading north toward High Gate.

Passing Box C, he saw a lone rider galloping toward the posse's camp on the creek. In the starlight,
he believed he recognized that slim figure as Texanna Conroy. The girl was heading toward the
bridge, no doubt to help plead Roy's cause with the
sheriff.

Reaching the foothills an hour later, Roy halted
to let Trigger rest, his eyes and ears keening the
night.

Was Bronc Alamar ahead of him? He heard no
sound of hoofbeats.

Dawn's early light was staining the ruins of
Haunted Mission with crimson when, two hours
later, Roy Rogers gained the north ridge overlooking Tomahawk Basin.

Daylight revealed no trace of Señor Rattlesnake's
band anywhere on the Basin floor. They had had
plenty of time to reach this hide-out on the divide,
but Roy saw no horses or men around the ruined
Spanish chapel.

Approaching through the mesquites from the east,
Roy left Trigger when he was within a hundred
yards of the mission. Not until he spotted a group
of saddle horses and mules hidden inside the mission
itself did he realize that Señor Rattlesnake and the
smuggler band were waiting for him here.

Roy's eyes flashed with excitement as he returned

to Trigger and there, concealed in the dense brush, put on the Ghost's skull mask and skeleton costume.

Then, mounting the palomino, he spurred out of the thorny jungle of mesquites and sent a hail toward the mission.

Instantly a serape-clad Mexican appeared in one of the windows of the bell tower where Señor Rattlesnake had posted him as a lookout.

"The Ghost is here, *señores!*" came the sentry's low-voiced cry.

By the time Roy Rogers reached the rear of the ruined building, Señor Rattlesnake and his men led their horses out into the open, trailing the loaded pack mules.

Roy Rogers's gutteral Spanish issued from behind his skull mask. "Why is it, *amigo,* that you waited out here? Why did you not go directly to the Well of Bones as I instructed you?"

Señor Rattlesnake eyed the masked man quizzically.

"Are you forgetting," he said, "that you have not told us that secret? None of us has ever seen your Well of Bones."

Roy grunted in secret dismay. It had not occurred to him that the Ghost of Mystery Rancho had not shared the location of the padres' tunnel with his partner, Señor Rattlesnake.

"Come with me, *señores,*" the fake Ghost said.

Roy Met Señor Rattlesnake's Gang

"We are not safe out here. At the Well of Bones we will be."

Dismounting, Roy led Trigger into the thickets which furred the ridge behind the mission, closely followed by Señor Rattlesnake and his men.

A moment later they came in sight of the cunningly concealed doorway of the tunnel which the friars of long ago had dug as a means of escape in case of Indian attack.

The smuggler band followed eagerly as Roy led the way into the gloomy underground passage, obviously relieved to reach this place of safety.

The sun's direct rays had not yet reached the hidden canyon at the other end of the tunnel when Roy Rogers led the outlaws into view of the tumble-down Spanish barn. Señor Rattlesnake and his men stared around at this cliff-walled hide-out, grinning with approval. No Texas lawman knew of this lair; they would be safe here.

"The Well of Bones," Señor Rattlesnake spoke up, unable to curb his curiosity. "It is here, *amigo?*"

Roy Rogers turned to face the outlaws whom he had led into this trap.

"The Well of Bones is beyond the barn," he said, gesturing with his arm. "You are all tired and sleepy from your long ride. You can unsaddle now, and unload the pack mules. You will find plenty of room in the barn to bed down."

Roy turned to Señor Rattlesnake.

"I will go back to the mission," he said, "and keep watch throughout the morning while the rest of you sleep, just in case any riders come this way."

Señor Rattlesnake grinned. "It is *bueno*," he said. "We are all nearly dead for rest."

While the smugglers busied themselves unloading the pack mules, Roy Rogers headed back toward the tunnel. His plans were working perfectly. All he had to do now was close the outer door of the tunnel and wait for Sheriff Stockton's men to arrive at Haunted Mission. With luck, the posse would find Señor Rattlesnake and his men sound asleep.

Reaching the dark opening of the tunnel, Roy reached under the Ghost's disguise to consult his watch. Six-fifteen. He had an hour and three quarters to wait outside before Tommy Stockton's posse showed up, according to plan.

In the act of stepping into the gloomy mouth of the tunnel, Roy Rogers caught sight of a shotgun muzzle aimed directly at his stomach protruding from the shadows there.

Frozen with surprise, Roy Rogers gasped as he saw the stocky figure which held that shotgun—a figure clad in a skull mask and skeleton costume identical to his own disguise.

He was caught under the drop of the *real* Ghost of Mystery Rancho!

CHAPTER XXIII

UNMASKED IMPOSTOR

A yell of astonishment went up from the ranks of the smugglers behind Roy Rogers as they saw two identically dressed masked men facing each other at the cavern mouth. One of the "Ghosts" held a shotgun on the other. The latter—the mystery rider who had brought them here from Mexico last night— stood with spread fingers poised over his six-gun butts.

Boots hammered on the flinty floor of the canyon as Señor Rattlesnake and his men hurried to where the two identical Ghosts stood.

"What is this?" shouted Señor Rattlesnake, dismay making his voice tremble. "There are not *two* Ghosts of Mystery Rancho!"

The real Ghost moved forward to shove his shotgun muzzle against Roy Rogers's stomach.

"You have been tricked by a fake Ghost, Señor Rattlesnake!" the real Ghost's voice came angrily from behind his skull mask. "This 'Ghost' who led you here is the Texas *Rangero,* Roy Rogers!"

The smugglers stared at each other in dismay.

"That cannot be so!" protested Señor Rattlesnake.

"Señor Rogers was thrown into the Well of Bones to die."

The Ghost laughed harshly. "He escaped. How, I do not *sabe*. Señor Rattlesnake, take off this impostor's mask. You will see that I speak truth!"

Desperation put an icy touch on Roy Rogers's spine. With an incredibly swift move, he thrust his hands forward and down, knocking the shotgun muzzle away from his stomach.

The Ghost jerked triggers, peppering the ground between Roy Rogers's wide-spread feet with buckshot.

Even as Roy's hands stabbed to his guns, Señor Rattlesnake leaped forward, swinging his own Colt like a club.

As Roy's Colts leaped from leather, the steel bludgeon smashed him across the temple and he sprawled to the ground, his senses reeling.

Snarling a Spanish oath, Señor Rattlesnake lifted his gun to cover the second masked man.

"We will solve this mystery soon enough!" snarled the smuggler king. "Mendoza, take off this man's mask!"

Roy Rogers was vaguely aware of rough hands rolling him over on his back. Mendoza reached under the skull mask and tugged it off Roy's head, revealing the cowboy's face for all to see.

"This cannot be so!" groaned the Mexican smuggler chief. "I am confused, *amigos*. Is it possible that a Texas Ranger brought us north of the Rio Grande to this place?"

The Ghost of Mystery Rancho opened the breech of his smoking shotgun, ejected the fired shell cases, and from a pocket of his chaps drew two more cartridges, which he slipped into his weapon.

"You have had a very narrow escape, *señores*," the Ghost told the goggle-eyed group of smugglers who were staring down at Roy Rogers. "This *Rangero* is wearing my extra costume, which I slipped into his saddlebags night before last, hoping to thus discredit Señor Rogers with the sheriff in Gunsight."

Señor Rattlesnake passed a trembling hand over his eyes.

"I see now," the smuggler king said, "why this fake Ghost said so many perplexing things. He assumed we knew how to reach the Well of Bones, for instance. I should have known. I have been very stupid, *amigo*."

Mendoza was busy stripping the black vest and chaps off Roy Rogers. The sun, peeping over the canyon rim at that moment, flashed blindingly off the Texas Ranger badge pinned to Roy's shirt.

Señor Rattlesnake, seeing that Roy was rapidly reviving, stooped down to take possession of the cowboy's twin six-guns.

"Why did he bring us to the Well of Bones?"

spoke up Mendoza.

The Ghost of Mystery Rancho laughed harshly. "This was to have been a trap, *señores*. Less than two hours from now, the sheriff and his posse from Gunsight will arrive at Haunted Mission. You would all have been trapped like rats."

Roy Rogers felt himself being hauled to his feet. He knew he was doomed; this gang of outlaws would kill him before making their own escape from Haunted Mission. With help not due for nearly two hours, Sheriff Stockton would reach the Spanish ruins and find them deserted. Unless the Gunsight posse stumbled onto the tunnel entrance by accident, they would never know the key to Roy Rogers's fate—until, sooner or later, Texanna Conroy would disclose the location of the Well of Bones.

"This time," he heard the Ghost saying, "we will make sure that this Ranger is dead. We must return to Mexico. And we can never use our tunnel under the Rio Grande again—Señor Rogers betrayed our secret to the world. For that, Rogers must pay."

Señor Rattlesnake said grimly, "Let us throw this impostor into the Well of Bones, Señor Ghost. Let him starve to death as the other lawmen starved."

The Ghost shook his head, his eyes flashing venomously behind his skull mask.

"Señorita Conroy knows where the Well of Bones is located and would rescue Rogers before he starved.

And a bullet in the heart is too merciful a revenge to take. No, *señores,* Roy Rogers must die, but it must be a painful death."

The smugglers were milling about nervously, anxious to get out of this canyon which, but for the opportune appearance of the real Ghost, would have been their death-trap today.

"We have plenty of time, *señores,*" the Ghost of Mystery Rancho said. "Tie this Ranger's legs securely. I have a plan. Señor Rogers will die—but he will live long enough to be sorry he masqueraded as the Ghost."

Still weak from the blow on his head, Roy was helpless as one of the smugglers brought a rope from one of the diamond-hitched pack mules and trussed his legs at knee and ankle.

Then Mendoza hoisted Rogers's bulk over a shoulder and followed Señor Rattlesnake and the Ghost back to the ancient Spanish barn.

Using the free end of the rope which bound Rogers's legs, the Ghost tossed the lariat over one of the heavy hayloft timbers of the barn.

Then, while the outlaws gathered around to watch, the Ghost laid his shotgun aside and seized the rope.

With Señor Rattlesnake's help, the helpless cowboy found himself hoisted off the floor of the barn and drawn up to the ceiling beam, hanging head-down by the ankles.

"This will not kill the *Rangero!*" protested Señor Rattlesnake, as he watched the Ghost anchor the rope to a wooden pillar which supported the hayloft. "You will put a bullet in his stomach before we leave him, no?"

The Ghost's laugh was like a reptile's hiss.

"Roy Rogers will be burned alive," the masked outlaw hissed. "We will leave this *Rangero* dangling upside down as you see him. Then we will set the hay in this barn on fire."

Swinging helplessly by the legs, Roy Rogers saw the upturned faces of the grinning outlaws below him. He saw the Ghost of Mystery Rancho fish in his chaps pocket for a match, saw the outlaw climb a heavy ladder to the haymow of the Spanish barn.

Striking the match, the Ghost tossed it into the tinder-dry straw, saw it burst into flame. Within minutes, this barn would be a blazing Hades. When the hayloft floor burned through, Roy Rogers would be buried under tons of flaming hay.

The Ghost of Mystery Rancho hastily retreated down the ladder, away from the fierce heat.

Rejoining Señor Rattlesnake and his henchmen, the Ghost stared up at Roy Rogers's dangling figure.

"*Adios,* Señor Roy!" jeered the masked killer. "You will be roasted alive by the time Sheriff Stockton reaches here. And by that time, Señor Rattlesnake and I will be well on our way to the Rio Grande and safety."

Already the roar of the blazing hay was deafening. Above that roar, Roy Rogers shouted the name of the man he knew the Ghost must be, but his words were lost in the crackle of flames.

Retreating outdoors, the Ghost shouted to his smuggler band. "To your horses, *amigos*. We must be far away from the Haunted Mission before the sheriff's posse arrives. I am sorry we cannot linger here to watch Roy Rogers die."

Through the open door of the barn, Roy Rogers had his upside-down view of the outlaws as they hastily led their horses out to the tunnel.

The pack mules, panicked by the smoke and flame of the blazing barn, stampeded after the escaping outlaws, leaving only Roy Rogers's faithful palomino behind.

Frantically, Roy Rogers tried to double his body so that he could get a grip on the rope tied to his legs. With his hands free, he knew he had a chance to untie his ropes; but reaching them he found was impossible. Señor Rattlesnake's vicious blow on his skull had left Roy Rogers as weak as a new-born calf.

Having tied Trigger, the Ghost of Mystery Rancho took his last look at the blazing barn, and then headed into the tunnel, through which Señor Rattlesnake and his men had gone.

CHAPTER XXIV

ONE-MAN BRONCO

When the Ghost emerged from the far end of the tunnel he found Señor Rattlesnake and his henchmen already in saddle, out in the clearing behind the Haunted Mission.

"My horse is picketed out in the brush, *señores!*" the Ghost yelled. "We must be sure to keep out of sight under the skyline until we are well away from this spot."

Heading eastward toward the chaparral where he had concealed his mount, the Ghost had not taken a dozen steps before the morning quiet was blasted by the roar of a .30-30 and a bullet streaked through space to pluck a slot through the masked outlaw's sombrero crown.

Spinning around, thinking that Señor Rattlesnake or one of his men had fired a traitorous shot at him, the Ghost beheld an appalling sight.

Charging around both ends of the Haunted Mission came a group of mounted riders, heading straight toward Señor Rattlesnake and his band of mounted outlaws!

In their lead was Tommy Stockton, the courageous

young sheriff from Gunsight. Stockton had brought his posse to the mission a good hour and a half ahead of schedule!

With hoarse yells of horror, the Mexican smugglers jerked out their guns to return the blistering fire of the Gunsight posse riders.

The Ghost turned to sprint toward the chaparral for cover, screaming bullets buzzing like wasps around him.

A pitched battle was being enacted down on the flat behind the ruined mission, as the posse closed in to surround Señor Rattlesnake and his trapped smugglers.

Dust and gunsmoke blended to obscure that scene as the Ghost slogged up the slope toward the tunnel leading to the Well of Bones.

Dimly through the swirling dust, the Ghost saw the Mexican bandit king, Señor Rattlesnake, knocked off his saddle by a hailstorm of bullets.

Jerking his six-guns, the Ghost laid his own answering shots at the milling posse riders, saw one Gunsight man hurl high his arms and pitch from saddle. Tommy Stockton, the one target the Ghost most wanted to hit, was lost in the pandemonium of the surprise attack.

A bullet struck the Ghost's spiked boot heel, knocking him off his feet. Another burned a streak across his shoulder, feeling like the stroke of a red-hot branding iron on his flesh.

With frantic haste, the Ghost picked himself up and vanished into the mesquites.

He heard posse riders spurring their horses into the brush after him, as he reached the open door of the tunnel.

In the darkness he found a big iron bar used to lock the doorway from the inside, and got it in its sockets. Nothing short of axes or dynamite would open that tunnel door now.

The Ghost of Mystery Rancho was gasping like a landed fish when he staggered out into the smoke-filled canyon.

To his left, the Spanish barn was a mass of flames, part of its roof already having caved in on the blazing haymow. When the fire had eaten through the loft floor it would cover Roy Rogers under tons of flaming débris.

The Ghost did not head toward the barn. His objective now was Roy's fast saddle horse, Trigger.

Groping through the dense smoke, sparks and blazing straw pelting his sombrero, the Ghost of Mystery Rancho located Trigger, prancing nervously alongside the juniper snag to which the Ghost had tied him.

Clawing at the rein knots with trembling fingers, the Ghost unloosened Trigger, set foot to a stirrup, and vaulted into Roy Rogers's silver-mounted saddle.

Then he reined Trigger around, pointing him down-canyon toward the secret getaway trail leading out of this gorge.

But the Ghost had not reckoned on the fact that Trigger was strictly a one-man bronco.

Before he had taken a dozen paces under the strike of the Ghost's sharp spur rowels, Trigger suddenly swapped ends like a bucking horse in a rodeo arena.

A skilled rider who had topped more than one man-killing bucker in his lifetime, the Ghost was caught by surprise by Trigger's change of direction, and one boot was thrown out of stirrups.

Grabbing the saddle horn, the Ghost felt Trigger's back suddenly arch like a bursting spring. The palomino landed with a jarring crash on all four hoofs, closely bunched, at the same time jerking the reins out of the Ghost's hands as the horse "swallowed his head."

Sunfishing and rearing, Trigger sent the Ghost of Mystery Rancho hurtling through space. The outlaw landed heavily on his back and lay there gasping, too weak to roll away if Trigger decided to follow up with stamping steel-shod hoofs.

Through a rift in the choking smoke clouds inside the barn, Roy Rogers had his inverted view of Trigger's bucking off the outlaw.

Putting fingers between his teeth, Roy Rogers gave an ear-splitting whistle.

The Ghost Hurtled Through Space

Instantly Trigger seemed to forget his vengeance on the man who had spurred him so cruelly.

A second time Roy Rogers whistled, and Trigger wheeled around and headed straight for the blazing barn.

Into the smoke-pouring mouth of the barn door the loyal palomino charged, ignoring the red tongues of flame which were licking up the spilled hay on the barn floor.

Squarely under the dangling, upside-down figure of his master, Trigger halted.

With frantic haste, Roy Rogers clawed at the straps of a saddlebag with his dangling arms. Out of that leather pouch he clawed a bowie knife in its sheath.

Summoning his last ounce of strength, Roy doubled his body upward against the pull of gravity, bracing one hand on Trigger's saddle horn.

With that much leverage, Roy made his swipe at the ropes binding his legs with the razor-whetted bowie knife.

A moment later the ropes snapped and Roy fell headfirst against Trigger's withers, landing on the smoldering straw of the barn floor.

While Trigger snorted in panic beside him, Roy cut the remaining ropes which were still wrapped around his legs, kicked himself free and came to his feet.

There was no need to grab Trigger's reins and lead him out of this blazing barn. Horse and cowboy raced out of the barn door side by side.

They were not ten feet from the doomed building when the fire-gutted haymow gave way with a resounding crash, completely filling the barn's lower floor with seething hay and burning timbers.

Staggering through the rolling smoke and sparks, Roy Rogers saw the dim figure of the Ghost of Mystery Rancho coming to his feet.

The Ghost's guns had spilled from holsters when Trigger had bucked him off, and the masked outlaw was gazing about frantically in search of those weapons now, as he saw Roy Rogers reeling toward him out of the blazing inferno of the collapsed barn.

Roy's yell was lost in the deafening thunder of the flames behind him as he charged the Ghost.

Locked in a grapple, Roy and the masked outlaw crashed to the ground and rolled over and over. The Ghost's powerful hands were trying to lock a strangling grip on Roy's throat, his nails clawing ribbons of skin from Roy's neck.

Hammering the Ghost's face with both fists, Roy saw the bright stain of blood spreading on the cloth skull mask.

They came to their feet and broke apart, slugging toe-to-toe, exchanging vicious rights and lefts, neither feeling the sting of the other's fists.

The Ghost had a superior reach and he out-weighed Roy Rogers, but the latter's boxing skill evened the odds. Like a saloon brawler, the Ghost ducked his jaw to his chest and charged in behind flailing fists, bawling low in his throat like an en-raged bull.

Roy halted the Ghost's attack with a looping hay-maker to the jaw which snapped the masked man's head back on his shoulders. Before the Ghost could cover up, Roy stung his temple with a left jab and followed up with a smoking uppercut to the chin.

That last blow, landing with meaty impact with every ounce of Roy Rogers's fighting power behind it, told the story. The snakelike eyes behind the Ghost's mask glazed over, and he fell backward like a sledged steer.

Gasping breath into his lungs, choking from the hot smoke which filled this canyon, Roy Rogers stood over his vanquished enemy, while Trigger hovered in the background.

Then, reaching down, Roy Rogers ripped the skull mask off his unconscious foe, to stare down at the face of the Ghost of Mystery Rancho.

"My hunch was right," Roy Rogers said huskily, flinging the bloodstained mask aside as he stared at the bruised visage of the insensible outlaw at his feet. "You are no more a blind man than I am, Jingo Bates."

CHAPTER XXV

THE GHOST'S SECRET

In the shadow of the Haunted Mission, Sheriff Tommy Stockton and his victorious possemen were riding herd on the four surviving members of Señor Rattlesnake's gang who had surrendered rather than face the certain death from the posse's guns.

Señor Rattlesnake lay dead at their feet, riddled with bullets. And among the dead was a man who had burst from the surrounding chaparral during the middle of the fight, to lend his aid to the trapped outlaws.

That man was Bronc Alamar, the cavvy wrangler from Box C. Now that it was over, Sheriff Stockton knew that Alamar had been a member of the smuggling band, and had left the posse's camp down on the Lizard, riding here to warn Señor Rattlesnake's gang of their impending danger.

Bronc Alamar had arrived too late. He had died before the flaming guns of the Gunsight posse a few moments before the survivers had surrendered.

Standing at the sheriff's side was Texanna Conroy, who had insisted on accompanying her future husband to this gunsmoke showdown at the mission.

"It's lucky I decided to get here earlier than Roy Rogers ordered us to," the sheriff said. "Five minutes later and we wouldn't have seen hide nor hair of Señor Rattlesnake's bunch."

The girl was staring at the column of white smoke lifting above the ridge north of the mission ruins.

"We've got to get to the Well of Bones, Tommy!" the girl said desperately. "That's where the Ghost was heading. That's where Roy must be."

A few minutes later Texanna had led Stockton and five of his possemen to the locked door of the tunnel.

Stockton lifted his rifle nervously as he heard the sound of a metal bar being lifted, inside the door.

The door opened, to reveal Roy Rogers, his face blistered and his eyebrows singed off clean, standing in the doorway of the tunnel. The cowboy who wore John Whetlaw's Texas Ranger badge was supporting the skeleton-costumed bulk of the Ghost of Mystery Rancho.

"*Jingo Bates!*" cried Texanna Conroy, as she recognized the unmasked outlaw. "Why—he can't be the Ghost, Roy,—there's been some terrible mistake. Jingo is blind—"

Roy Rogers shook his head.

Turning to the scar-faced foreman of the Box C spread, he said to the battered foreman, "Tell Texanna and the sheriff what you told me, Jingo."

Trigger moved up out of the smoke-filled tunnel to nuzzle Roy's shoulder as Jingo Bates looked squarely into Texanna's eyes.

"I'm not blind," he said. "I got burned severely around the eyes when an oil stove exploded over at Señor Rattlesnake's lair, but I didn't lose my eyesight. I—I pretended to be stone blind so no one at Box C would suspect I was the Ghost."

Texanna turned to Roy Rogers.

"You told me at the house last night," she reminded him, "that you knew the identity of the Ghost. You thought he was Bronc Alamar, didn't you?"

Roy grinned. "For a while I thought Bronc was the Ghost. But I got to thinking of a lot of little details which I had overlooked before.

"For instance," Roy said, "remember the time you and Jingo saved me from the quicksand bog? Why was Jingo Bates so near the scene? You thought he was out riding. In reality he was returning to the ranch after letting us see him in his Ghost costume. It was Jingo Bates who put dummy bullets in my guns at the bunkhouse the first night I came to Box C—so I would think the Ghost was bulletproof."

Jingo Bates's nod confirmed Roy's words.

"Going back to the beginning," Roy went on, "it was Jingo who picked up John Whetlaw's telegram saying John would meet your father here at the mission. Jingo planted that fake message in the can under the Painted Rock, and it was Jingo who manipulated the Talking Skull and murdered John. I saw him making his getaway wearing one of Box C's scarlet rodeo shirts.

"The thing that really made me suspect Jingo might not be blind, however," Roy continued, "was the planting of his extra Ghost costume in my saddlebags the other night. Remember how you fed me supper, Texanna, and Jingo left the house? He went out to the barn where I'd left Trigger and put the Ghost costume into my saddlebags then. Then he rode to town and slipped that message signed 'A Friend' under the sheriff's door. I got to thinking about things when I was cooling my heels in Stockton's jail cell."

As they walked down to the Haunted Mission to rejoin the rest of the posse, Jingo Bates had his look at the dead bodies of Señor Rattlesnake and Bronc Alamar.

"Bronc worked with me," Jingo said. "I told him to kill Roy Rogers over at the Skeleton Canyon line-camp cabin. Bronc's dynamite trap failed. It was my rifle that kept Roy pinned down while Bronc made his escape that night."

Texanna Conroy stared at the foreman, hardly able yet to realize that he had masqueraded so long as a blind man.

"But why—why?" the girl asked. "Why did you assume the role of the Ghost, Jingo? Why did you try to destroy Box C?"

Jingo Bates grinned, his battered lips puffed and swollen from Roy Rogers's hammer blows.

"It started one day when I was visiting these ruins," Jingo Bates said, gesturing at the Haunted Mission. "I found an old map of Tomahawk Basin in there, drawn by the padres hundreds of years ago. It revealed the location of the tunnel under the Rio Grande which the padres had built—"

"And which I blew up with Bronc Alamar's dynamite," interrupted Roy Rogers, "only last night."

Jingo Bates shrugged hopelessly. "I saw what an ideal route that tunnel would make for smugglers," the crooked foreman continued, "so I contacted Señor Rattlesnake and we went into partnership."

Sheriff Stockton snapped a pair of handcuffs over Bates's wrists.

"And you became the Ghost so as to scare everyone off Box C?" Stockton asked.

Jingo nodded. "Yes. I wanted to frighten Buck Conroy into selling me the ranch. Posing as a blind man, I'd pretend to operate Box C. With Furtado Gomez printing counterfeit money and with Señor Rattlesnake smuggling in the rice paper by way of our tunnel, I'd have been a millionaire soon."

Jingo Bates turned to Texanna.

"I'd hoped," he said, "to win your love, Texanna. I'd take a trip to New York and return with my eyesight restored, and I'd hoped you'd marry me. When I realized Stockton had won you—well, that's why I was going to let you die with Roy Rogers in the Well of Bones."

Tommy Stockton said in a merciless voice, "You'll be hanged for your crimes before Texanna and I are married, Jingo. Now that Roy Rogers has laid the Ghost of Mystery Rancho, old Buck can make Box C prosper again."

Roy Rogers reached up to unpin his Ranger badge.

"I'll stick around for the wedding," he told Tommy and the girl, "and then I'll return to San Antonio to present John Whetlaw's Ranger badge to his widow. My job is finished here—I've fulfilled the oath I gave to my dying friend." He turned to Jingo Bates as a new thought struck him. "How'd you happen to come up to the mission today, Bates?"

The exposed Ghost grinned. "I overheard your talk with Texanna at her window last night, from the living-room window in the opposite ell."

Sheriff Stockton turned to his waiting riders.

"We'll return to Gunsight with our prisoners," he said. "We all wanted to hang Roy Rogers as the Ghost. Before long we'll hear a judge and jury sentence Jingo Bates to the gallows."

Roy found himself alone with Bates as the others turned away.

"You proved yourself to be a better man than I, Roy," Jingo Bates said, in the utterly hopeless voice of a man who knew his jig was up. "I've cached a lot of smuggler loot here at Haunted Mission. I figure that to the victor belongs the spoils. Shall I lead you to where the gold and jewels are hidden?"

Roy Rogers smiled bleakly.

"All right, Jingo. I hadn't expected any favors from you."

They were walking along the front of the mission now, out of sight of the others.

"The gold cache is out in the brush where I shot Texanna's pinto pony the other day," Jingo Bates was saying as they approached the open portal of Haunted Mission. "Your Trigger pony ran off, Roy, or I would have shot that palomino of yours."

Jingo Bates, his Ghost costume gleaming in the sun, was walking ahead of Roy Rogers as they reached the mission doorway.

Without warning, the Box C foreman suddenly leaped sideways and landed with all his weight on the wooden threshold of the mission doorway.

Inside the ruined building there sounded the blast of an exploding six-gun, and before Roy Rogers's shocked eyes he saw his prisoner stagger to the drilling shock of a bullet in the chest.

As Jingo Bates pitched into the weeds in front of the door, Roy stared into the murky opening.

Smoke wisped from the barrel of one of the headless skeleton's guns. In that moment, Roy realized that Jingo Bates had recocked the six-guns of the Talking Skull, and that by jumping on the threshold board he had jerked the wires leading to the hair triggers of the mummy's guns.

Staring down at the dead body of the Ghost, Roy Rogers shook his head slowly. He reached in his pocket to finger the Texas Ranger star he would return to John Whetlaw's grieving wife in San Antonio.

"Well, friend John," the cowboy whispered sadly, "it looks as if the Ghost tricked me here at the very end. He used the same murder trap that killed you to end his own lawless career."

Hoofbeats drummed around the mission's campanile as Tommy Stockton and Texanna Conroy galloped around to the front of the ruins, to investigate the sound of the gunshot.

They reined up there, staring aghast at the prone body of Jingo Bates.

Roy Rogers reached for Trigger's reins.

"Yes," Roy Rogers said, "Jingo Bates has cheated the gallows with a suicide bullet. The Talking Skull wrote both the start and the finish of the story of the Ghost of Mystery Rancho."

WHITMAN BOOKS
FOR BOYS AND GIRLS

NEW STORIES
OF ADVENTURE AND MYSTERY

Up-to-the-minute novels for boys and girls about favorite characters, all popular and well known—

ROY ROGERS and the Rimrod Renegades
ROY ROGERS and the Gopher Creek Gunman
ROY ROGERS and the Raiders of Sawtooth Ridge
ROY ROGERS and the Outlaws of Sundown Valley
ROY ROGERS and the Ghost of Mystery Rancho

GENE AUTRY and the Big Valley Grab
GENE AUTRY and the Bad Men of Broken Bow
GENE AUTRY and the Thief River Outlaws
GENE AUTRY and the Redwood Pirates
GENE AUTRY and the Golden Ladder Gang

TARZAN and the City of Gold
TARZAN and the Forbidden City

THE BOBBSEY TWINS: Merry Days Indoors and Out
THE BOBBSEY TWINS in the Country
THE BOBBSEY TWINS at the Seashore

WHITMAN BOOKS
FOR BOYS AND GIRLS

NEW STORIES
OF ADVENTURE AND MYSTERY

THE WALTON BOYS in High Country
THE WALTON BOYS in Rapids Ahead
THE WALTON BOYS and Gold in the Snow

SAND DUNE PONY

RIP FOSTER Rides the Gray Planet

TOM STETSON and the Blue Devil
TOM STETSON and the Giant Jungle Ants
TOM STETSON on the Trail of the Lost Tribe

GINNY GORDON and the Mystery at the Old Barn
GINNY GORDON and the Mystery of the Missing Heirloom
GINNY GORDON and the Disappearing Candlesticks

TRIXIE BELDEN and the Gatehouse Mystery
TRIXIE BELDEN and the Red Trailer Mystery
TRIXIE BELDEN and the Secret of the Mansion

ZANE GREY'S The Spirit of the Border
ZANE GREY'S The Last Trail

**The books listed above may be purchased at
the same store where you secured this book.**